I0618233

The Ghost Witch's Dagger

Trevor Finlay

Published by Trevor Finlay, 2025.

THE GHOST WITCH'S DAGGER

First edition. July 21, 2025.

Copyright © 2025 Trevor Finlay.

ISBN: 978-0646721132

Written by Trevor Finlay.

For my wife Michele

My kindest critic and biggest fan.

A friendship forged in magic

Chapter One The Dagger

I run as fast as I can down the slippery, dark backstreet. Rain gushes along a central gutter, funneled by the overhanging eaves of the two-story buildings. Behind me, boots pound the pavement. Voices shout.

"Stop, thief!" one of them yells.

They must have seen me bolt. I spot a narrow alley between buildings and dart into it, nearly losing my footing. I keep going, fingers skimming along wet stone until I find a tight gap. I turn sideways, squeeze through—and luck is with me. The passage opens up into a narrow corridor of shadow.

"Where did he go?"

"Don't know. It's black as pitch in there."

I hear them fumbling in the dark, groping at the walls.

"Where are you, thief?" As if I'd answer.

"I think he gave us the slip. Let's keep moving."

Their footsteps fade into the storm.

Crouching low, I fight to steady my breath. Carefully, I pull the jeweled dagger from my tunic. In the dim trickle of light, the golden hilt gleams, studded with dull red gems. Maybe I can fence it. Maybe it'll keep the hunger at bay.

A low growl rumbles beside me.

I freeze.

Only now do I notice the mound of fur, large and breathing slow and deep. "At least you didn't squash my tail," says a voice—inside my head.

I stare. The dog stares back.

I can hear you, I think, uncertain.

A second growl. This one wary.

I slowly extend my hand, offering my scent. A cold nose probes the air, then brushes my fingers.

"Hmph. You're as hungry as I am," says the voice. "You had meat two days ago."

I reach again, fingers trembling, but a sharp growl halts me.

"Did you squeeze in here too?" I ask, thinking the words more than speaking them.

"For the same reason," comes the gruff reply. "Except I had a chicken."

"Too fat to get out?"

"Not anymore. It passed through."

I sniff. A faint sour stench lingers deeper in the alley.

We sit in silence for a while, side by side in the dark. The dog shifts, then gently nudges my hand. This time, I touch its head. My fingers sink into warm, thick fur at the neck. A quiet bond stirs—slow, steady, like rain easing after a storm.

Eventually, I rise. Reaching up, I find a ledge, pull myself up, and stretch. The dog stands, stretches long and low, front legs then back. Overhead, a sliver of sky glows—the first hint of dawn.

I slip out into the alley, moving quickly away from the scene of last night's theft. A flicker in the corner of my eye makes me stop.

No one there.

I glance down. The black dog sits at my feet, tail tapping the ground like an impatient human foot.

"You following me?"

"Nothing better to do."

"Alright. Let's go."

We brave the wide and waking Main Street. Wagons rattle by, hooves clatter. The scent of rain mingles with rising bread. Vendors sweep their stalls and greet each other. Barrows overflow with fresh vegetables, fruit, and meat.

We skirt the town square and head toward the canal, where barges unload crates and voices bounce off the stone walls. We pass beneath a low footbridge. Drunks snore in the shadows of lean-tos. A sagging collection of crates and tarps form a shanty village nearby.

Among the clutter—an old wagon wheel, split timbers, broken furniture—I spot a man slouched in a battered chair. He watches me approach. One eye squints directly at me. The other drifts somewhere behind my shoulder.

"Pierre," he says, standing. "What've you got?"

"Hello, Squint."

I pull the dagger from my tunic. Its jeweled handle flashes in the dim morning light.

Squint whistles low. "That's fancy. But hard to move. I can't give you much."

"Whatever you think is fair."

He digs into his coat and counts out ten copper coins. I pocket them. Hunger drowns my caution.

I head back toward the square, stomach growling. The smell of roast pork hooks my nose. A huge man sits on a bench with an iron cashbox chained to it.

"How much for a lower leg joint?" I ask.

"Five," he grunts. He catches me eyeing the box. "Touch it and I'll break your arm."

I hand him five coins and take the meat. With the rest, I buy a crusty breadstick and a large juicy apple.

At the fountain, I sit and eat. Steam rises from the meat. My stomach settles.

Drool pools near my feet.

The dog stares.

I slice the bread, stuff in the last strip of meat, and hand him the bone. He takes it and trots off.

The voice in my head is gone.

I drink from the fountain, then cross the footbridge. On the opposite bank, Squint waves at me. I wave back.

I find a quiet spot beneath a weeping willow. I finish the apple, lick juice from my fingers, and drift into sleep.

A sharp kick on the sole of my foot jerks me awake.

A huge man stands over me, blocking the sun.

"I want a word with you, boy," he says, yanking me to my feet. He waves the jeweled dagger in front of my face. "Seen this before?"

"No," I lie, struggling in his grip.

"Funny. Your friend over there says different."

I look toward the bridge. Squint leans on the railing, flipping a gold coin. He pockets it and strolls off.

Bastard.

The peacekeeper sneers. "Looks like you've got some explaining to do, sonny." He clamps a hand on the back of my neck and marches me away.

Shame burns in my chest. People jeer. Someone spits at my feet.

The lockup rises ahead—a squat, grim building with a crooked stable on one side and a mess room tacked on the other.

The peacekeeper shoves me through the door into a cramped foyer. Wooden benches line the walls.

A short man with a potbelly and a rodent face stands up.

"Lord Glamier," the peacekeeper says. "Here's your stolen property—and your thief." He gives me a shake, like I'm a game animal he just caught and killed.

"Shall we?" he says, opening the inner door.

Lord Glamier nods.

We go inside.

Chapter Two Consequences

"Throw, you thought you could steal from me, did you?" lisps Lord Glamier, trying to look down his nose at me.

I glance down, shaking my head, biting my tongue to stifle a laugh.

Too late—he's already seen the grin I failed to hide.

"Oh, you think it's funny, do you?"

"No," I say, reckless now. "I've never met a talking rabbit before."

The peacekeeper beside him snorts before quickly stifling it, eyes darting nervously to Glamier.

Glamier's nostrils flare. His lips peel back in a snarl, showing every inch of those oversized, yellowed buck teeth.

"How dare you inth-ult me!" he screeches, his voice rising to a shrill whine. "Pea-th-keeper, hold hi-th hand down. I'll teach thi-th brat a leath-on."

The peacekeeper doesn't hesitate. His hands are iron as he slams me chest-first onto the table, wrenching one arm behind my back. My other hand is pinned, palm-down on the scarred wooden table.

"Wait—" I twist, heart hammering, breath catching in my throat. "You don't have to—"

The dagger flashes. Glamier draws it with a flourish, letting the lamplight dance along its edge. My stomach knots. I can't look away.

"Thieves, get, marked," he hisses, stepping closer.

Then the tip kisses my skin.

It's cold at first. Just a whisper of metal. Then it bites.

A sharp line of pain streaks across the back of my hand as blood wells up. I grit my teeth hard enough to crack one. My vision blurs.

He pauses. Looks me in the eye.

Then he presses harder.

I suck in a breath as the blade carves deeper, slower. He's not cutting—he's etching. My skin peels back in a thin red line as he drags the blade downward, turning the cut into a shape. A letter.

My legs go weak. I want to scream, but I won't give him the satisfaction.

He finishes with a flick of his wrist and steps back like a proud artist, holding the dagger up effeminately.

"In ca-th you didn't know," he says, beaming, "that is the letter, tee, for thief. Thatch what you are."

The pain pulses, deep and hot. I clench my jaw, but a grunt slips out as fire lances through my hand.

I taste copper. Realize I've bitten my tongue.

The peacekeeper lets go of me, grabs the back of my collar, and throws me into an empty cell. The door slams shut behind me with a final clang.

"Wait, I wrath not finished!" Glamier protests.

"Apologies, my lord," the peacekeeper says. "But we don't usually torture petty criminals in this town."

"I own thi-th town!" Glamier squawks.

"Not all of it, my lord." The peacekeeper gestures toward the door. "Unless there's more business?"

With an outraged huff, Glamier raises his nose and storms out.

A voice calls from the adjacent cell. "What a despicable, inbred twat. You alright in there?"

"I'll live," I mutter.

"Name's Jack."

"Pierre."

"Well met, lad. That Glamier family's got a lot to answer for, y'know."

"I don't know much about them. Just that they own all the land in and around the town."

"You never heard of Falandor Glamier? Crusader and founder of this town?"

"The name rings a bell. That's all."

Jack leans closer to the bars. "Then I've got a story for you."

"Four hundred years ago, Falandor came back from the crusades with a wagon full of stolen gold, gems, and rare goods. Built the church spire and bell house to glorify the spread of Christianity. People flocked to the village for work and peace, and never left.

He built the castle up on the ridge. Took a young wife, wanted an heir. She died in childbirth. Married again, found real love, and had three daughters—but still no son.

When his wife became pregnant again, he prayed for a boy. She died giving birth to another girl. That broke him. Turned bitter. Started drinking. Ignored the fourth daughter—sickly, quiet. Blamed her for his wife's death. Then came madness. He convinced himself his eldest daughter was his dead wife reborn. Obsessed. She bore him a son. He was ecstatic. The others, jealous, did the same. Each one gave birth to sons, all carrying the Glamier name.

To stop the infighting, Falandor divided the land between the boys. The daughters built great Houses and left him to rot.

Only the youngest stayed. She nursed him, kept him alive well past a hundred. Had a gift for animals, they say. After his death, she lived alone in the ruined castle, crafting exquisite jewelry and weapons with the blacksmith's help.

Rumors of witchcraft spread. Her nephews came with torches, saw her work, killed her for it, and burned the castle. Claimed she'd attacked them and accidentally set the fire herself."

"Is that story true?" I ask.

"As true as my family line. My ancestors helped build that castle."

"So why are you in here?"

"Sometimes I drink and talk too much about the Glamier family. Next thing I know, I'm accused of blasphemy and tossed in here."

"And the priest goes along with it?"

"They pay his wages."

"So they really do own the town. And some of its people."

"You've got it, lad. Where you from?"

"Mill Town. Two towns up the canal."

"What brings you here?"

"My father died in a mill accident. Mother succumbed to sickness. I'm trying to make a new start."

"Well, good luck in this town. You'll need it."

The peacekeeper returns with a bucket of hot water and two mops. "Here's the deal, boys. Clean the cells, and you're free to go."

I'm up in a flash. Jack, slower, eyes him suspiciously.

"What's the catch?" he asks.

"If you don't, you stay another night. Festival starts today—it'll be busy."

I'm already scrubbing the first cell.

"Hey son," the peacekeeper calls. "What's your name again?"

"Pierre."

"I'm Robert. My brother runs a restaurant on the square. He needs help—cleaning, feeding the fire, scrubbing pots. Interested?"

"Yes, sir."

"Finish here, and I'll take you to meet him."

Jack sloshes water half-heartedly.

"No wriggle room, Jack. Half the work or no deal."

Half an hour later, I'm done, waiting on the foyer bench, wounded hand throbbing.

"Let's go," says Robert, walking so fast I jog to keep up. I glance at the wound. "What about this?"

"Say it happened at work," he says, handing me a folded rag. I tie it tight as we enter the restaurant.

"Julian," Robert says, hugging his brother. "Found a worker for you."

Julian looks me over. "Do what I say, when I say, fast—and we'll be fine."

"Yes, sir."

"Say 'yes, Chef.'"

"Yes, Chef."

"Good. Get a clean bandage, then bring in firewood."

"Yes, Chef. Where are the bandages?"

"I'll show you," Robert says, leading me out back. He wraps my hand himself, then shows me the woodpile.

I spend the rest of the day sweeping, stacking wood, wiping benches—working around cooks and servers as they flow in and out.

That night, Julian pays out copper coins to the staff. When he gets to me, he hesitates.

"Robert told me what you did. Don't ever steal from me." He pauses. "You got a place to stay?"

"No, Chef."

"You hungry?"

"Yes, Chef."

He hands me a plate of leftovers, then a candle.

"You can sleep in the woodshed. Be up first thing."

I nod and clear a spot among the firewood. The sawdust and chips make for a surprisingly soft bed. I snuff the candle and sleep deeply.

Morning comes with a rooster's cry and pale light filtering through the shed slats. I wash, peel off the filthy bandage, and inspect the wound. Still tender, but healing. I'm already waiting at the back door when Chef Julian arrives.

The days blur—shopping trips, sweeping, firewood, cleaning. Two weeks pass. The air turns cold. I save enough for a blanket and warmer clothes.

One morning, the wind kicks leaves into spirals across the square. I wheel the barrow toward Ivan's stand. Today, beside his usual goods, a pig sleeps behind his bench.

"Hello, Pierre!" he booms. "How are you?"

"Well, thanks. And you?"

"Happy today," he grins.

"What's new?"

He pulls a small, dark, knobbly ball from a box. "Sniff."

I lean in. "Smells like forest floor. Mushrooms. Earth."

"Yes!" he beams. "Wonderful, isn't it?"

I nod, unsure.

Then—hoofbeats. A buggy screeches into the square. A dog is tied to the back, yelping as the driver leaps out and starts whipping it with a horse switch.

It's Roger Glamier.

I storm up and grab the switch from behind. He spins, eyes bulging.

"You rabid rabbit," I spit.

"How dare you!" he screams.

"How dare you beat that dog!"

A crowd gathers. I cut the dog's rope. It bolts through the square. The same black dog who once spoke to me.

Roger grabs the switch, yanking. I let go. He stumbles backward, falls flat. Laughter erupts.

Red with rage, he lashes out. Ivan steps between us, looming.

Roger scrambles into the buggy, whips the horse. It bolts. My wheelbarrow is in its path—splinters fly.

Ivan shakes his head.

I gather what's left of the wheelbarrow and head back to the restaurant.

Julian glares at me. "Did I tell you to get involved out there?"

"No, Chef."

"But you did it anyway. Roger Glamier dines here. Spends money. If I keep you, he'll go elsewhere. Might do that anyway.

You're fired. Pack your things. Don't come back."A few minutes later, I'm standing on the edge of the square with nothing but a small bundle of belongings and nowhere to go.

Chapter Three The Forest Shadow

I see Ivan watching me, so I walk over.

"So, Chef Julian let you go?"

"He did. Now I've got nowhere to go."

"Well, Pierre, remember that truffle I showed you earlier? Want to help me find more? I've got a small pig farm on the edge of town. You can sleep in the hayloft."

"Oh—yes, please, Ivan. Thank you."

He laughs at my eagerness and claps me on the shoulder.

We pack up his stall after the morning trade, harness his pig, and trundle slowly out of town.

"Ivan," I say, "do you know the Glamier family history?"

"Oh, that old story? What of it?"

"Did the fourth daughter really make jewelry and talk to animals?"

Ivan chuckles. "Maybe. I think it's been exaggerated. But there's said to be a dagger with gems in the hilt."

"I've heard that too," I lie. "Do you believe magic exists?"

He shrugs. "Maybe. If you want it to. But I wouldn't count on it."

We pass Roger Glamier's sprawling house.

"Big house for such a small man," I mutter.

Ivan chuckles. "Don't let him get to you."

Eventually, we reach a small stone cottage with a garden out front. A track runs past the right side, leading to a barn. Pig pens line the bottom, with a hayloft above.

We pen the pig and head inside through the back door. A plump woman stirs a pot on the stove.

"Hello, Dorris," says Ivan, kissing her cheek. "This is Pierre.""Hello, Pierre. Are you hungry?"

"Always," I grin.

The three of us share a hearty bowl of stew. Ivan tells Dorris about my day—saving the dog, losing my job, and helping him find truffles.

"Well, young man," she says with a smile, "you've got a treat ahead of you."

"I'm sure I do. Thanks again, Ivan."

He chuckles, deep and warm. "You might not be so thankful this time tomorrow."

Just then, a whining cry drifts in from outside. I open the door and find the black dog from earlier. He's limping, holding up a paw.

"Oh, the poor thing," Dorris says. She returns with a bowl of stew. The dog waits for us to step back before he eats. Ivan fetches empty sacks and makes a bed for him against the cottage wall.

"That Glamier—" I start.

"I know how cruel he is," Ivan interrupts. "But you can't win. Best avoid him."

I pick at the healing scabs on my hand and nod.

"Did he do that to your hand?" Dorris asks, shocked.

I nod again. A heavy silence settles over us.

"A good night's sleep is all we need," Ivan says. "The moon's up. Take your things to the hayloft, Pierre. We head to the forest at first light."

"Thanks for the stew. Goodnight."

I climb the ladder, nestle into the hay, and fall asleep quickly. Before dawn, a cold wind wakes me. I burrow deeper and wait for warmth to return. As the sky lightens, I climb down and head for the house. The black dog is curled on his sack bed, eyes on me. As I approach, he lifts his head. I give him space and sit on the back step. He rises, pads over, and sits in front of me. Together, we greet the new day.

Ivan opens the door. I step aside. He looks at the dog and grins.

"Looks like you've found a friend, Pierre. Come in for breakfast."

I bring in firewood.

"Thanks, Pierre," says Dorris, cracking eggs and tossing bacon in a pan. She spots the dog and prepares a bowl—eggs, cold meat—and hands it to me. I set it down.

"Go ahead," I say. He waits, then devours it.

We sit to scrambled eggs and bacon with grated truffle.

"This is delicious," I say.

Dorris and Ivan exchange a look, then smile.

"It's a gift from Mother Nature," Ivan says. "We'd best get moving if we want more."

At the barn, Ivan fits the pig with a different harness—leather straps with handholds. Dorris appears with a backpack.

"Thanks, sweetheart," Ivan says, kissing her cheek as he shoulders it.

"Good luck, boys," she calls.

We walk past pastureland where horses and cows graze. At a crossroads, Ivan points.

"South leads through farmland. North to the ruined castle. But west—into the old oak forest—is where we're headed."

We follow a path lined with old stumps and young saplings competing for light. The road climbs alongside a trickling brook. As it levels out, the trees grow taller, their autumn leaves clinging stubbornly. Red, gold, and brown drift in thick layers across the forest floor. Moss covers the exposed ground and climbs the trees. The air is fresh, the breeze gentle, and the scent of sun-warmed leaves fills my lungs.

Ivan stops beside a fallen log, drops his pack, and wipes sweat from his brow. The black dog sits nearby, watching us.

We continue, the pig in the lead. Her nose swings side to side, then digs into the forest floor. Ivan grabs the harness, halts her, and points. I dig and uncover a large truffle. The pig gets a potato reward, and Ivan pockets the find.

We repeat the process. Ivan's pockets bulge, and he runs out of potatoes.

The dog begins sniffing the ground, zigzagging. He stops, paws the dirt, and looks at me. I dig—another truffle.

We return to Ivan, who raises an eyebrow. He adds it to the haul and hands me a steel pot to fetch water. I find a still pool and catch sight of myself—my boyish features gone, replaced by a face beginning to grow a beard.

Another face appears—furry, curious—over my shoulder. My shadow.

"Hey Ivan, I thought of a name for the dog."

"Oh? What is it?"

"Shadow."

He nods. "Good name. In here, no one has a shadow."

Ivan builds a fire. From his pack, he pulls bread, cheese, cold meat. We eat in silence. When the water boils, he stirs in coffee grounds and lets it brew.

"Good work today," he says, pouring mugs.

"Thanks. I really enjoyed it. I like the forest."

"And you showed me something new. Or rather, your dog did."

We drink, then head back. The sun hangs low in a quiet, windless sky.

At home, Ivan lays out the truffles. Dorris cleans them gently, brushing off dirt, washing them, then drying and wrapping them for market.

"Pierre, you deserve a break. Go to the tavern—have a few drinks." Ivan presses some coins into my hand.

"Thanks." I head into town, passing Chef Julian's restaurant. Roger Glamier dines with his wife—a round woman with small eyes and tight curls. A man in black sits with them. I don't recognize him.

I keep walking to the smoky, noisy tavern, order a brew, and find a quiet corner. The noise grates on me, and the drink warms my head too fast. I decide to leave.

Outside, night has fallen. As I walk, I glance back—and see a man in a long black robe with a wide-brimmed hat gaining on me.

I stop, heart pounding. He shoves me into a doorway, pulls a knife, and presses it to my throat.

Chapter Four The Priest

"I saw you the other day, mocking my friend and benefactor, Lord Glamier," says the man. His mouth is thin and mean, recessed into his face like a scar. A hooked nose juts over bulging eyes that leer on their own, as if possessed.

"What of it? He was beating a tied-up dog."

"I don't care about that. He can do whatever he likes. This is your first and last warning," he says, pressing the knife harder against my neck.

"Alright. I'm sorry—I won't do it again."

"Not good enough," he growls.

"What do you want from me?"

"If you were a few years younger, I'd have a different answer. But no—I want you in church tomorrow. Ready to repent. If not, the next time we meet like this will be the death of you."

"Yes, alright—I'll be there. Please, let me go," I whisper, each breath feeling like it could be my last.

"You can tell anyone about this little conversation. But they won't believe you." He smiles grimly. "My name is Father Andre. And there's only one you should fear more than me."

He brings his hands together in mock prayer, crosses himself with a muttered blessing, and strides back down the street.

I stand there, trembling. My fingers find the thin line of blood on my neck. I hurry back to the stone cottage, my mind spinning.

"Hello there—you're back early," Dorris says quietly as I slip inside. Ivan dozes in an easy chair by the fire.

I nod and sit, staring down at my hands.

"Everything alright, Pierre?" she asks, gently lifting my chin.

She gasps and pulls back at the sight of the thin bloody cut on my neck.

My eyes blur with tears as I bite my lip. Dorris wraps me in a warm embrace.

"What did I miss?" Ivan stirs, rubbing his eyes.

Dorris answers for me. "It looks like our young lad has been attacked."

"No! Who did this?" Ivan demands.

I blurt out the whole story. They listen, mouths agape, eyes wide.

"Well, Dorris," Ivan says at last, "looks like we're all going to church tomorrow."

"I've never been to church," I admit.

"Don't you worry, love," Dorris says, winking at Ivan. "We'll look after you."

"Alright. I'll get to bed, then. Goodnight."

"Goodnight," they say together.

Outside, I sit with Shadow, scratching behind his ears. Then I climb to the hayloft, trying to sleep, but my mind won't stop. Father Andre came for me—sent by Glamier. All over a bruised ego. My life now hangs by a thread because of that petty, rabbit-faced tyrant.

I lie still, but the rage churns. I get up and go for a walk.

I take the dark back lanes toward the center of town, soon standing at the back gate of the Glamier mansion. I know the way. This time, I move without sound or hesitation.

I return unnoticed, the dagger tucked into my tunic.

Back in the hayloft, I burrow down to the floorboards and wedge the dagger into a narrow gap between wall and floor. They'll blame me, sure—but without proof, they can't touch me. Serves that smug bastard right, I think, smiling as sleep finally takes me.

Morning comes with the first winter frost, creeping across the fields and stone streets. I wake cold, wrapping my blanket tighter as steamy breath floats before me.

Climbing down to the crunchy ground, I'm met by Shadow. I scratch behind his ears, down his back, finishing with a rub at the base of his tail.

Aah, that feels good, rumbles a voice inside my head.

I freeze. "Talking again?"

Never stopped.

I stare at him, stunned. The dagger. Of course. It lets me hear him.

What a fool I was to give it up.

"Hey Pierre, you coming in for breakfast?" Ivan calls from the back door.

I say nothing about the dagger and join them inside. The scrambled eggs and bacon with fresh truffle are as delicious as ever.

"You ready for church?" Dorris asks.

"I suppose I am," I reply, with a worried glance.

"Let's get it over with," says Ivan, rising.

We follow the tolling bells down the main street. More villagers join the quiet procession. The church is a large, timber-framed building, beams and trusses arching high above us. Stained-glass windows line the sides—men in robes doing noble deeds. At the front stands a wooden cross with a tortured man nailed to it.

I hope that's not my future—then realize it's just a statue.

The crowd settles. Murmurs fade.

Father Andre appears, climbing the lectern. He sings and chants from a great book, before stepping down and signaling a robed man at the pipe organ. Music begins, then a choir. Andre joins in.

Then he returns to the lectern and begins a furious tirade about sin, damnation, and roasting in hell. As his voice rises, so does my hatred for him.

The service drags on—music, more singing, a collection bag passed around. I watch in disbelief as coins drop in. My head aches from the absurdity of it all.

Finally, it ends. We file out. Father Andre stands at the exit, shaking hands.

Ivan grabs his hand, crushing it. The priest winces and drops to one knee.

"Thank you, Father," says Ivan, sweetly. "Especially the part about 'do unto others as you'd have them do unto you.'"

Following his lead, I shake Andre's hand—firm and fast. A tear slips from his eye.

We walk back toward the farm.

"So, Pierre—what did you think of church?" Dorris asks.

"It's... unbelievable," I say, vaguely.

Ivan chuckles. "You're not wrong."

The Glamiers speed past in their buggy, nearly clipping a group of children. I say nothing, but I want to scream. Then I remember the dagger, and I smile.

We spend the rest of the day quietly. I throw a stick for Shadow, Dorris tends her flowers, and Ivan potters in the yard. For a while, everything feels calm. But I know it won't last.

Chapter Five Accusations

A cold northerly wind whistles down the valley through the forest as I descend from the hayloft to face the day.

"Hey boss, I'm going rabbit hunting," Shadow calls, trotting away before I can reply.

I watch him vanish into the trees, then push open the back door. The warm, fragrant scent of breakfast draws me inside. Dorris and Ivan are already seated, and soon I'm sharing another delicious meal with them.

"Come to the market with me this morning, Pierre. I could use your help," Ivan says.

"Alright, let's go."

We hitch the pig to the cart, loaded with roasted pork, potatoes, and a box of truffles, and trundle into town. The market square is bustling—voices rise, deals are struck, crates are unloaded, coin exchanged. Within an hour, half the truffles are gone.

That's when I see them: Robert the peacekeeper, with Roger Glamier at his side.

I shrink into the shadows behind the cart, but Robert walks straight toward me. I step out, trying to appear nonchalant, knowing there's no use hiding.

"Pierre, come out here. I want a word with you."

"What is it, sir?" I ask, keeping my voice even.

"Don't pretend to be inno-thent," Glamier snaps.

"Please, let me handle this, my lord," says the peacekeeper.

"I have no idea what this is about," I lie, feigning indignation.

"The dagger's been stolen again. I need to search you."

"Go ahead." I turn, place my hands on the cart, and widen my stance. He frisks me thoroughly, empties my pockets—nothing.

Then Glamier shrieks.

Shadow has his teeth sunk deep into Glamier's calf, shaking viciously. Blood pours down into his shoe. The peacekeeper tries to kick him, but Shadow slips away into the crowd. Glamier collapses, eyes rolling back in his head.

Robert scoops up his limp, bloodied form and carries him toward his brother's restaurant, leaving a crimson trail behind.

The market stares, stunned. Slowly, the chatter returns, like waking from a spell.

"What was that?" Ivan asks, bewildered.

"Revenge, I guess." I shrug.

"You might be right," Ivan says with a chuckle, turning back to barter with another customer.

By midday, we've sold nearly everything. We pack up and head along Main Street toward the farm. On the way, we pass a man pushing a gurney. Glamier lies atop it, pale and woozy, swaddled under a blanket. Robert walks beside him, grim-faced.

Back at the farm, I chop firewood while Ivan unhitches the pig. A few minutes later, he reappears wearing his best tunic and a coin pouch heavy with earnings.

"Come on, Pierre," he says, striding past. "We're going to pay the rent."

"To Glamier?"

"His relative. The Glamiers descend from three sisters—each built their homes around the village."

"Well, better than seeing old Rabbit-Face."

Ivan chuckles. We turn down the south road. Ahead, a stone bridge comes into view. Three men loiter there—Shadow growls.

"Hello, Pierre. Got any more ornamental daggers for sale?" says Squint, grinning crookedly.

I pat my tunic. "Sorry, sold the last one."

"Word is you gave it away for a few coppers." I bite my tongue and keep walking. Laughter trails behind us.

"What was that about a dagger?" Ivan asks.

"He cheated me, that's all."

"Figures. That one would steal from a baby."

We approach a wrought-iron gate draped in roses. Past it, a curved, tree-lined driveway leads to a grand stone house. Ivan knocks. A tall, black-clad man answers.

"Hello, Ivan. How may I help you?"

"I'm here to pay my landlord, Travis."

"Very well. Please wait inside."

The foyer is vast. A glass display case stands against the wall, filled with curious trinkets—gemmed cups, ornate vases, and, at the center, a silver stag's-head amulet with emeralds and ruby eyes.

Lord Gerard enters, elderly and stooped, leaning on a cane. His face is long, horse-like, his eyes a faded blue.

"Hello Ivan. And who's this?"

"This is Pierre, my farmhand."

"Hello, Lord Gerard."

"Oh, just Gerard, please. At my age, formality wastes time I don't have."

A girl appears beside him—my age, unmistakably his granddaughter. Her smile is disarming, luminous.

"This is Annmarie," Gerard says.

"Hello," she says with a graceful curtsy.

"Hello, Annmarie. I'm Pierre."

My hand starts to itch. The scar on the back of it burns hot. I clasp both hands behind me, trying to ignore it.

Ivan hands over the rent pouch. After polite farewells, we step outside.

By the time we return to the farm, the scar has turned red and swollen, with a yellowed center.

"What's wrong with your hand?" Ivan asks.

"I don't know... it feels poisoned."

"Dorris will fix it."

I nod, distracted. "Where are Annmarie's parents?"

"They died by the canal, summer before last. A draft horse broke free and killed her mother. Her father tried to help—he never woke up, lingered for weeks before dying."

"I know how she feels. My parents died around the same time."

"Oh, Pierre... I didn't know. Is that why you came to Falandor?"

"Yes. I couldn't stand the empty sympathy. I was starving, and all they gave me were hollow words. So I left. Jumped a barge. Ended up here."

As we near the bridge, Squint and his friends leap off. On the canal below, they begin rifling through cargo. Whatever they're doing, I know it's dishonest—and profitable.

Robert the peacekeeper waits by the farm gate, hands on hips.

"Pierre! I want a word."

"I'm listening."

"That dog of yours needs to be destroyed."

"Why? Because he bit a man who tried to kill him?"

"I could bite him too," Shadow growls.

I ignore him.

"Come on, Robert," Ivan says. "Look at him—he's not aggressive."

"He's dangerous. I'll be back in the morning. Have him ready, or I'll arrest you too."

He turns and walks away.

My chest tightens. Shadow, my only friend—gone?

Inside, Dorris gasps when Ivan relays the news.

"That's terrible. So unfair," she says.

"I think you need to leave town for a while," Ivan says.

"Where would I go?"

"There's an old workers' lodge by the quarry."

"Can we go now?"

"I think we should," Ivan agrees.

"Food first," Dorris insists.

We eat quickly. Ivan packs a duffel; Dorris wraps bread, cheese, and cold meat. I climb to the loft, retrieve the dagger—hot to the touch—and wrap it in cloth before stuffing it in the bag.

Night is falling. We head into the forest, Shadow leading the way. He vanishes and reappears in moonlit patches of road.

"You know," Ivan says, "you've got worse luck than anyone I've met."

"It's not luck. Glamier's trying to ruin me."

"You provoke him."

"Maybe. But fate seems to throw us together."

"Fate or choice—both ripple through the lives around us."

"If I disappear, will he forget me?"

"If you want to live, disappearing's your best choice."

We walk in silence.

"When will you hunt truffles again?"

"Tomorrow. You know where."

The road climbs, pine replacing oak. A waterfall marks a sharp turn, then the road climbs up to a high saddle. We ascend a steep section of road lined with pines and reach the quarry. The solid stone lodge is bathed in moonlight squatting next to the dark water of the quarry lake. Shadow drinks, shakes off, and trots into the darkness eager for a new adventure.

"Let's get a fire going," Ivan says, opening the door. Inside, it's bare: two beds, a long table, a hearth.

I climb into the fireplace, peer up. "Blocked chimney. Back in a sec."

Outside, I find a dead pine branch, bring it in, and jab it upward. A pile of soot and needles crashes down on me.

Ivan laughs. "You look like your dog."

Shadow pads up beside him. "Not furry enough. Hahaha."

I wash in the lake. When I return, Ivan has a small fire going.

"Use dry wood only. Smoke will give you away."

On the table are supplies: a cooking pot, an axe, and a crossbow.

"This was my grandfather's. Use it, but take care. Don't lose the bolts."

"Thank you. I'll look after it."

Ivan nods. "I have to go. Sleep well."

"Good night."

I close the door. By the fire, I stroke Shadow until we're both drowsy. I spread my blanket, and the dagger clunks to the floor. I place it on the table and lie down.

That night, I dream.

A castle atop the ridge.

An old woman in white robes, hair billowing in the wind.
She wears the stag amulet and hand-feeds a wild deer.

Sunset clouds morph into wolves, then rabbits, pigs, horses, dragons.
Darkness falls.
And the White Lady remains—
Wind-blown,
Ghostly,
White.

Chapter Six Murderous Morals

The unfamiliar, dim-grey stone room challenges my tormented memory, pushing me to remember where I am. Slowly, the sequence of events pieces itself together as a wet tongue licks my face awake.

I swing my legs off the side of the bed. Shadow, my loyal companion, watches me with bright eyes. I reach out and rub the sides of his furry black neck.

"Good morning, boss," says Shadow, his voice low and gravelly.

"Good morning, Shadow." I realize how little we've spoken, yet how much we've shared without needing words.

I rise and empty the duffel bag onto the table. I unwrap the food Dorris kindly gave me the night before, and gratitude warms me. At the bottom of the bag, I find a small empty pouch and tie it to my belt. I cut into the smoked pork leg, preparing bite-sized chunks. Some I eat, the rest I feed to Shadow and store in the pouch. I slide the dagger into the inside pocket of my tunic and head down to the lake for a drink and a wash.

We follow the west road into the oak forest, reaching the fallen log where we'd hunted truffles with Ivan a week ago. Down to the stream, across it, up the opposite bank—ancient oaks greet us, their gnarled limbs like frozen storms.

Shadow begins sniffing and pawing through the leaves.

"What have you got?"

"Truffle," he says simply.

"Good boy." I hand him a piece of pork.

I uncover the dirt with a stick, dig deeper with my dagger, and lift out a truffle the size of my fist. As we return to the log, Ivan approaches from the road.

"Morning, Ivan."

"Morning," he grumbles.

"You alright?"

"I'm fine. I just don't like lying."

"Oh—you mean Robert?"

"And Father Andre. He's a bloodthirsty bastard."

"He was going to kill Shadow?"

"In front of us. I told them you'd gone back to Mill Town."

I hold up the enormous truffle. Ivan's frown transforms into a grin.

"Pierre, this almost makes up for it."

"I found it across the stream."

"Go fill the pot. I need coffee."

When we return, Ivan has a fire going. Shadow and I go back out and return with six more truffles. Ivan laughs when he sees them.

"I didn't feel like finding truffles today—and now I don't have to. Thanks, Pierre. Next time I'll leave the pig behind."

We sip hot coffee in silence. Ivan hands me dried fruit—bitter coffee, sweet fruit, perfect harmony.

He gives me a bundle of herbs. "If you kill a deer, use these to smoke it. A few green pine branches help too. Do it overnight—less chance the smoke will be seen."

"Thanks, Ivan. Want more truffles?"

"Same again would be perfect."

We cross back. Shadow finds six more. I reward him, pocket them, and return.

Ivan bags them, then pats his knees. Shadow bounds over, tail wagging, soaking up ear scratches and a rough pat on the head.

"Good boy, Shadow."

"Thanks, boss," Shadow pants, grinning.

Ivan nudges his pig. "Best be going."

"When will you be back?"

"Few days. I'll come to the quarry."

The sun has crept past midday. We climb toward the hairpin turn by the waterfall. Water rushes beneath the road through a stone drain. I drink, wash, then we hike briskly up to the quarry's saddle. Pine needles line the roadside, forming a narrow footpath. Through the trees, far below, I glimpse the twisting road and cascading falls.

We reach the quarry lodge. The door hangs open. I could've sworn I closed that, I think.

I step inside—and freeze. Shadow halts beside me, teeth bared, snarling.

Father Andre sits at the table, crossbow aimed and loaded.

"You're a long way from Mill Town, boy," he sneers. "Ivan's a terrible liar. I thought you'd be hiding here." He leans forward, places a knife on the table. His eyes glint with smug satisfaction. "First, I kill your mangy mutt. Then you're jailed. Then... well, your cellmate Jack is a bore. He dies. And then you, a thief, murderer, and owner of a dangerous beast, will hang."

"Why?" I ask.

"My job is to protect the innocent—from monsters like you."

He lifts the crossbow and takes aim at Shadow.

Then he sees it.

His eyes widen. The bolt flies—past Shadow—and clatters outside.

A white figure hurtles toward him, passing through the table.

Andre shrieks, topples backward, scrambles like a spider, flips over, and flees out the door—ghost in pursuit.

I chase. He slips on pine needles—gone. He tumbles off the cliffside, his descent punctuated by thuds, cracks, and a final sickening silence.

We race down. His body lies mangled, but breathing.

"Help me," he croaks.

"You're dying. I could make it quick."

"I want to live."

"I can't help you."

"Damn you," he spits, coughing blood. His body convulses, then falls still.

From the corner of my eye, I see him—his ghost, grinning beside me.

"I can't die. I have the most important job in the world. Ha! Ha!"

I point to his corpse. His grin fades. Shadows thicken. The waterfall roars louder. Darkness creeps toward him.

"No!" he screams.

They seize him—drag him into the base of the falls. The sound recedes, like water swirling down a drain. Silence returns.

The vile soul of Father Andre is gone.

I won't wait to be accused. I rush back to the lodge, pack in the fading light. I find Andre's knife and toss it over the cliff.

Shadow and I follow the road toward the castle. The moon rises—yellow and wide—over broken stone. The rusted portcullis above the gate resembles the maw of a long-dead beast.

We slip inside. I rest against the cold wall. Shadow curls close.

What if the priest had succeeded? I shudder.

We move into the guard tower. I wrap myself in a blanket behind the battlements, I doze off and dream of the White Lady again. Voices jolt me awake. I peer down from the battlements and spot Robert and Ivan in a heated argument.

"I told you, Robert, he went back to Mill Town."

"What about the dead priest, then? How do you explain that?"

"Obviously, he slipped off the road and fell."

"Did he fall—or was he pushed?"

"Good question. Still, coming up here is a waste of time. You can search the castle on your own. Everyone knows it's haunted."

"You people are so superstitious," Robert mutters and strides under the portcullis. A moment later, I hear a surprised grunt. He storms back past Ivan without stopping. "I've had second thoughts. Let's go."

Ivan glances up at me, smiles, and waves before following Robert down the hill.

I descend the stairs in the guard tower and cross the courtyard to the great hall. As I step inside, I freeze—standing before me is the White Lady. But this time, she's smiling.

"You have my old dagger," she says.

I'm speechless, staring at the translucent figure before me. Shadow wags his tail, clearly delighted, as if greeting an old friend.

"Are you Falandor Glamier's fourth daughter?"

"I was. You may call me Emelda."

"Did you make the dagger and the amulet?"

"I did, but the magic came from a powerful wizard who lived with me in the castle during my final years."

"What happened to him?"

"He moved on, after enchanting all three pieces of jewelry."

"There's a third?"

"Yes. The magic in the amulet and dagger clash. We created the Balance Ring to keep them from destroying each other."

"Where is the ring now?"

"In the cave beneath the castle. It used to be part of the drainage system."

"How do I get there?"

"There's a narrow ledge beneath the main gate that descends to a crevice in the rock face."

"Can you show me tomorrow?"

"I will—but only if you help me take revenge on the Glamier family so I may finally rest."

"It would be my pleasure," I say.

"Very well, young man. Get some sleep. Tomorrow, we set in motion a series of events that will ignite a new dawn for Falandor Town."

Chapter Seven Terror Traverse

The wind howls through the stone walls of the ruined castle. I wake up warm, curled around Shadow. Stretching out, I lean against the wall, dig into my bag, and eat the last of the pork with some bread and cheese. Shadow accepts a few treats and wanders off, nose twitching.

I head to the front gate and peer over the cliff. Below, I spot the narrow ledge Emelda mentioned. The rock face beneath is sheer, pine treetops swaying ten meters down. The stonework is weathered, with small gaps between blocks. I begin my descent slowly, carefully.

My feet touch the ledge while my hands still cling to the top. Panic surges—my grip locks. I force myself to breathe. One hand at a time, I shuffle sideways, my fingertips searching for holds between the stone blocks. It's working—repetition and rhythm carry me forward.

Then the ledge disappears.

I glance down—it's further below. I shift my hands, squat on one leg, and stretch the other to find the ledge again. The wind lashes at me, threatening to rip me from the cliff. I press on, edging around a bulge where the stone juts out. The ledge narrows.

Ahead, a vertical crevice marks the entrance. The ledge vanishes beneath me where the stone foundation has collapsed. Blocks have shifted, leaving foot-sized gaps. I wedge my boots between them and edge across.

Halfway, the block beneath me drops slightly. I freeze—then quickly move. Just in time, I find the ledge again and cling to it as the loose stone plummets, crashing through the forest below.

I hold tight, eyes closed, heart pounding, relief washing over me.

At last, I reach the corner where the stone wall meets the cliff. I squeeze through the gap and into the fissure.

Inside, the space widens enough to move freely. Patches of silty sediment mark where water once flowed. I begin searching, scraping through hollows, checking each carefully. After a while, I stretch, glance back toward the daylight—and something gleams above me.

I reach up and retrieve a gold signet ring. An 'ess' is carved through the center of the round face. One teardrop is inlaid with emeralds and a single ruby; the other, rubies with a single emerald. I pocket the ring.

Looking up, I see faint light at the top of a rough chimney. Rather than risk the ledge again, I climb and emerge in a small, partially roofed courtyard.

I take out the ring to inspect it—and nearly drop it.

"You found it!" Emelda's voice startles me.

"I could've used a hand," I mutter.

"Oh, I'm sorry. There's only one thing that scares me more than heights—tight spaces."

"But you're a ghost. You can't die."

"Doesn't mean I don't get scared," she says with a dramatic huff, gliding off with her nose in the air.

Back in the great hall, I sit down and try on the ring. The world shifts—everything blurs. I look down. My body is gone. I can't breathe.

I yank the ring off and gasp, air flooding back into my lungs.

"It's not a bad ring," Emelda says. "Use it with the amulet, and you'll be invisible for as long as you want."

"Well, I'd better go get it then."

"Yes, please. Then we can set the plan in motion. I've waited so long for this."

"Why are you afraid of heights and small spaces?" I ask gently.

"My sisters used to lock me in cupboards—sometimes for days. And they'd hang me by my ankles over the walls."

"That's awful. No one stopped them?"

"No. Father was always drunk or indifferent. So I wandered the forest. Nature became my comfort."

I need water. My throat is dry. I say goodbye, grab my crossbow and bag, and head to the quarry. Shadow's already there, lapping at the cool water. I drink deeply, then we walk to the lodge.

The place is a mess—signs of a struggle everywhere. I get to work. Mattresses go outside to dry, benches are stacked, and the floor swept. The routine reminds me of working in Chef Julian's restaurant. I wonder how he's doing.

Outside, I find a rope and pulley system under the eaves by the chimney—perfect for skinning game. Doris's meat-smoking herbs are still stored in the firewood rack.

"Shadow, let's go get some fresh meat."

"Alright, boss. You lead—I'll stay behind. That weapon scares me."

"You're a smart dog."

The terrain here's too steep, so we head to the saddle to find a game trail. Shadow picks up fresh droppings quickly. Luck is with us—a small herd of deer is upwind. We creep closer. I load the crossbow.

A clean shot to the heart. The deer drops, and the herd scatters.

I heft the carcass over my shoulders and carry it to the quarry. At the butcher's rack, I string it up, slice its throat, and let the blood drain before heading to the lake to wash.

I've watched butchering before. It doesn't take long to break the animal down. Shadow gnaws on a leg as I stack firewood and light a small, smokeless flame. The day fades into night.

Using the iron rack over the fire, I roast one of the back legs. When it's ready, I set it aside, stoke the fire high, and sit to eat. Fresh venison, a warm fire, and my dog beside me, chewing his bone in bliss.

The rest of the meat goes on the rack with smoking herbs spread over the coals. I turn everything once, then curl up for the night, ready for what tomorrow may bring.

Chapter Eight The Magic Combination

Cold, grey morning light invades the stone lodge. The smell of smoked venison lingers in the air as I stretch and look out into the crisp winter landscape. I wrap the venison into two parcels—one for Ivan and Dorris, and the other I leave in the lodge for another day.

"Shadow, I'm going to see Ivan and Dorris. You stay here."

"Okay, boss," he replies, ears drooping. Then he exhales through his lips, issuing a typical canine expletive.

I run down the hill past the waterfall and toward the crossroads. At the fork, I take the east road and walk the rest of the way. Nobody sees me as I circle around the back of the familiar stone cottage and knock on the door.

"Pierre," Ivan says, quickly ushering me inside.

"Hello, Dorris," I greet her.

"Oh, Pierre, it's so good to see you," she says, pulling me into a warm embrace.

"You know it's risky coming here," Ivan says.

"I know. I left the dog at the quarry lodge."

"We've got some bad news. Do you remember Gerard Glamier? He died in his sleep yesterday."

"Oh... well, he was very old."

"He was, but now Roger Glamier and his cousin Bartholomew inherit his holdings."

"What about Annmarie?"

"I'm afraid for that poor girl. She'll have to do whatever the Glamier cousins want if she wants to stay in her home."

"And a snake has a better moral compass than those two," Ivan cuts in.

"Everyone knows about the Glamier family's history of incest," Dorris says, close to tears.

"That's terrible. Something needs to be done," I reply, anger rising in my voice. I keep the secret of Emelda and the Balance Ring to myself. Then I pull the smoked venison from my bag and hand it to Dorris.

"What's this, Pierre?" she asks, smiling as she unwraps the meat.

"Very nice, Pierre," says Ivan, picking up a piece and giving it the sniff and squeeze test.

"I appreciated the food you gave me the other night. This is my way of saying thank you."

"Well, thank you, Pierre. That's very kind. Now take some bread and cheese," Dorris says, handing me a bundle.

I take it with a smile, say goodbye, and start back up toward the quarry. As I walk, I can't stop thinking about Annmarie being seduced and blackmailed by that rabbit-faced creep. I have to do something about it. Tonight, I'll go to her house and find a way to make her feel safe—and at the very least, scare the wits out of Roger Glamier.

When I return to the lodge, I see Shadow resting on the doorstep. He spots me, saunters over with his head down and tail wagging. I give him a quick pat and head inside. The place feels more like home now, with food in the cupboard and some cleaning done.

I go up to the castle to find Emelda. I wander through the bare, empty rooms and try to imagine what this place looked like before the Glamiers looted and burned its interior.

"Did you get the amulet?"

"Not yet, Emelda. I wish you'd stop sneaking up on me like that."

"Oh, sorry. It's a well-worn habit—and it's amusing watching those brave men run away like little girls."

"Gerard Glamier is dead. I'm going to get the amulet tonight. Is there anything I should know?"

"Leave the dagger behind. Even with the Balance Ring, the amulet and dagger can create unpredictable effects on the wearer."

"Unpredictable how? Will I turn into a werewolf or something?" I ask, half-joking.

"Maybe. Or you might not survive." Her voice turns quiet and serious. A shiver runs up my spine. "I tried it once and didn't wake for two days. Shortly after that, the Glamier cousins came and killed me. I saw them coming and tossed the Balance Ring down the privy. That's how I knew where it was."

"I had a dream about you hand-feeding wild deer. Could you really do that?"

"Oh yes, that's the magic of the amulet. It magnifies the love—or hatred—you have for animals. If you love and respect them, they'll approach you without fear. Annmarie's mother was killed by a horse while wearing it. She thought of them as stupid, smelly beasts of burden."

"I heard that story. It makes sense now."

"Well... most people underestimate animals. For many years, they were my only friends. But with the amulet, they became my family."

"Why did you make the dagger?"

"To communicate with animals. It can do that—but it stops there. I learned a lot from its limitations."

"Thank you for explaining this, Emelda. If I'm going to get the amulet, I'd better go. I'll see you tomorrow."

I return to the lodge with her words replaying in my head.

"Shadow, I'm going back to town tonight. You can come—but stay out of sight. No biting anyone, no matter what happens."

"Okay, boss," says Shadow, tail wagging and a big grin on his face.

I'm already worried, but I have to trust him.

We make our way down the hill after sunset, reaching the crossroads as night falls. We follow the south road, cross the canal bridge, and soon we're walking up the tree-lined driveway. As the house comes into view, I spot Roger Glamier's horse and buggy. The front door is wide open.

"Stay," I whisper to Shadow.

I creep up to the house and slip into the foyer. I hear Roger droning on about property values and rent. I head straight to the display cabinet, take the amulet, and put it on. A sense of calm confidence washes over me. I slip on the Balance Ring and vanish.

In the sitting room, Annmarie lounges at the end of a long couch, a glass of wine in hand. Her eyes are glazed, half-closed. Glamier sits too close, pretending to care.

"Oh, my dear, you look tired. Here, lie down—let me take your wine," he says with feigned concern. He sets the glass on the table, lifts her ankles, and slides her legs along the couch. Her dress rides up. He starts to pull down her underwear.

I step behind him and smack the back of his head—hard.

He freezes, then spins around, scanning the room wildly. I backhand him across the face. He staggers back, eyes wide with terror. Then he bolts—out the door, into his buggy.

I climb in beside him. He whips the horse into a gallop. I snatch the switch from his hand and toss it into the darkness. The horse slows to a leisurely trot, ignoring his frantic slaps with the reins.

At the crossroads, he pulls the right rein to turn. I grab the left, forcing the horse to stop. Roger's crying now—like a child. I make a fist and punch him in the ear.

He squeals and leaps from the buggy, running down the road, screaming and sobbing like a little boy.

I let him go.

Climbing out of the buggy, I pocket the ring and comfort the frightened horse, who nuzzles me gently in return.

With Shadow close by my side, we walk back up the north road to the quarry lodge and spend the evening by the fire, eating smoked venison with bread and cheese.

Chapter Nine

The Funeral and the Bishop

I emerge from the lodge well after sunrise, yawning and stretching, and see Ivan lumbering up the road. He puffs his way up to me and stops, bending over with his hands on his knees as he catches his breath.

"Morning, Ivan. Good to see you."

"Good morning, Pierre," he puffs, straightening up and wiping sweat from his forehead with the back of his hand.

"Why are you in a hurry?"

"Funeral. Now," he pants. "Let's go."

"One minute," I say, running inside. I sweep the magic jewelry into the duffel bag and toss it up into the loft. I tell Shadow to stay, then dash out to catch up with Ivan, who's already left.

"Dorris got a new black suit for you. She wants you to come to Gerard Glamier's funeral."

"What about Robert the peacekeeper?"

"He's leaving town with his brother. They're heading for the big city on the coast."

"So, I won't get arrested?"

"Not today. And please—whatever you do—stay away from Roger Glamier."

"By all means, I will."

We walk briskly back to the stone cottage. Dorris has set up a small tub of warm soapy water on a chair out back.

"Wash now," she says and disappears inside with Ivan to give me some privacy. I peel off my smelly clothes and splash the warm water over myself, shivering slightly in the cold winter air. I towel off just in time for Ivan to appear from the back door with a black suit draped over his arm. He hands me a clean shirt. I put it on, then the pants, and finally the jacket. Dorris comes out with a hairbrush and a length of black ribbon. I sit while she brushes my hair back and ties it in a ponytail.

"Alright now, that's better. Let's go," says Dorris, walking away arm in arm with Ivan. I follow, my mind stirring with memories of past funerals—memories I'd buried long ago that now surfaced with fresh pain.

As we enter the church, I realize this funeral will be nothing like the muddy graveyard vigils I'd known. An exquisite, polished wooden coffin rests at the front. People file in and take their seats. Before long, the church is full. A man in a strange pointy hat and ornate robes appears beside the coffin.

"Oh, it's the Bishop," someone behind me whispers.

He starts in a manner reminiscent of Father Andre, offering platitudes about the generous and thoughtful qualities of the deceased before veering off-topic. He preaches the virtues of new technology, more money, and a better life for everyone in the great city by the ocean.

Eventually, he wraps up the service and calls for the prearranged pallbearers, who lift the coffin and carry it slowly from the church toward the small, ornate graveyard next door.

Dorris and Ivan find Annmarie beside the grave and support her in her tearful grief. Roger Glamier and his wife are present, along with the owner of the tavern, Bartholomew Glamier. I stand quietly, my emotional wounds prodded anew by the ceremony.

Across the street, a large wagon fitted with seats has a man standing on top, offering free transport to the city and a fabulous new life full of wealth and opportunity. A small crowd has gathered, murmuring and asking questions.

Dorris invites Annmarie to share a meal. The four of us return to the stone cottage and sit down to some of Dorris's best home cooking.

"This is very kind of you, Dorris. Roger Glamier dismissed my butler last night, and the house feels so large and empty now that I'm alone," says Annmarie.

"Why did he dismiss Travis?" Ivan asks.

"He gave me a reason, but I don't remember what it was. I fell asleep in the sitting room and didn't wake until early morning."

"I really think you need someone there to keep you safe," says Dorris.

"I agree," Ivan adds. "What if someone breaks in?"

"I know what you mean. The problem is, I have no money to pay anyone. Roger Glamier has taken financial control of my entire estate."

"I'd be happy to help out until you can make other arrangements," I offer.

"Oh, that's very nice of you, Pierre. But Roger Glamier told me you were a thief and couldn't be trusted. Is that true?"

"I made a mistake when I first came to town, but since working for Ivan, things have been much better."

She looks at me with a flicker of doubt. "I really don't want to upset my cousin—after all, he's my only source of income."

"Well, I still think you need someone to keep you safe," says Dorris.

"Could I ask you and Ivan to come and stay?" Annmarie asks.

"What about the farm?" says Ivan.

"I could take care of it for you," I offer.

"As a temporary measure, I suppose that will be fine," says Ivan with a sigh.

Relief washes over me as I recall stopping Roger from assaulting a drugged and unconscious Annmarie just last night.

"I need to grab a few things first. I'll be back before dark," I say.

"Not so fast," says Dorris. "You need to wash your clothes and get changed first."

I go outside and find my clothes already soaking in the tub. I wring them out and hang them in the sun to dry. Though it's cold, they're dry enough to wear after a few hours. While Annmarie and Dorris chat and clean the kitchen, I change and start walking back to the quarry lodge.

Shadow greets me with boundless energy, bounding up, tail wagging. I scratch behind his ears and give him long, affectionate strokes.

Inside the lodge, I climb to the loft and retrieve the duffel bag. I empty the jewelry onto the table and refill the bag with my spare clothes.

"You got the amulet!" says Emelda excitedly.

I nearly jump out of my skin. I wonder if I'll ever get used to her sudden appearances.

"I got it—and I scared Roger Glamier until he was crying like a child."

"Oh good. No one deserves a fright more than him."

It feels good to tell Emelda. I have to be cautious around Ivan and Dorris, but this secret is safe with the ghost.

I find a loose stone in the hearth, scoop out the powdered mortar, and hide the dagger in the recess. I don't want to risk activating all three pieces without knowing what might happen. I put on the amulet and walk down the hill with Shadow trotting happily at my side.

Back at the farm, Ivan and Dorris are preparing to leave for the night.

"You can sleep in the living room, Pierre. I've made up a bed for you," says Dorris.

"Thanks, Dorris. I'll see you in the morning."

Ivan clearly isn't happy with the arrangement and just grunts as he walks away with her.

Chapter Ten The Forest and the Fight

I rise early, take a walk along the south road, and meet Ivan coming the other way.

"Good morning, Ivan. How is Annmarie?" I ask.

"Morning, Pierre. Annmarie is talking about going to the city for a fresh start."

"It looks like a lot of people are interested in going."

"Come with me, Pierre. We need more truffles for the market tomorrow."

We return to the stone cottage. I wait outside while Ivan gets ready. Soon, we're walking along the west road without the pig. Ivan is unusually quiet, so I let him be. Before long, we reach the familiar roadside log nestled among the tall oak trees. A light breeze stirs the forest, and thick grey clouds overhead make it darker than usual.

Ivan takes a cloth bag from his pack and says, "Let's go. You and Shadow find them—I'll dig them up."

We cross the stream and climb into the old, majestic forest with its deep drifts of leaves and emerald moss. Shadow gets to work, finding a truffle within a minute. I uncover it, and Ivan levers it from the earth and drops it into the bag. We continue like that—one after another—until, without warning, Ivan stops.

He's staring at my chest. I look down and see that my shirt has come undone, revealing the amulet.

"That amulet belongs to Annmarie Glamier. What are you doing with it?"

"It's magical, Ivan."

"You stole it from her house. You should return it and beg for her forgiveness," he says, anger rising in his voice.

"Her mother died wearing this. Do you know why?"

"I know how her mother died!" Ivan shouts.

I decide it's best to show him. I reach into my tunic pocket, find the balance ring, slide a finger through it—and disappear. Ivan's jaw drops. He looks around wildly, trying to find me. I reappear. He staggers back and awkwardly sits on the ground.

"It's magic," I repeat, watching him carefully.

Ivan stares at me for a long time. Finally, he stands and says, "I don't know you anymore, Pierre. You're a thief and a liar—and now this... this magic. Who are you? What are you?"

"I'm your friend, Ivan. I never meant to hurt you or Dorris. Do you remember the night you saw me in the castle?"

"Of course I remember," he snaps.

"That night, I met the ghost who lives there. She told me where to find this ring." I take it out and show him.

He eyes it like it might bite. "Oh, Pierre. I don't know about this. I need time to think. Just stay away from me and my wife... Just stay away."

He takes his bag of truffles and leaves the forest without looking back.

The loss is heart-wrenching. How could I have been so careless as to let him see the amulet? I walk slowly back to the quarry lodge, gathering firewood along the way. My heart is heavy—like a cold stone. The more I think about it, the worse it feels. I sit on the front step and bury my face in my hands.

Shadow gently nudges me with his wet nose. I place my hands on his neck and look into his eyes.

"I love you, boss," comes the gravelly voice in the back of my mind.

"I love you too, Shadow," I whisper, a tear rolling down my cheek.

"I won't leave you alone," he says.

I wrap my arms around him and weep into his fur.

"Hungry, boss?"

It's the last thing on my mind, but somehow, my dog knows what I need.

"Let's go hunt a deer, Shadow."

I grab the crossbow, and we head to the saddle road. We shoot another deer. I process it like before, and we spend the afternoon and evening together, warm in the lodge, eating roast venison. We sit by the fire until we drift off to sleep.

Chapter Eleven The Haunted Tavern

"Pierre! Hey, wake up."

The first dim light of dawn seeps in, and Emelda is standing over me, beaming.

"What is it, Emelda?"

"I think it's time to make a plan for revenge on the Glamier family."

"What do you have in mind?"

"Well, you know how much they love money. What if they lost it all—left with nothing but the clothes on their backs?"

"I think that would hurt them more than death itself. But how do we do it?"

"I was hoping you'd have an idea."

"A lot of people are leaving town, so they'll collect less rent. That's a start, I suppose."

"No, too slow. We need to ruin them—quickly. Like a knife to the throat."

"Sorry, Emelda. I don't understand money any better than you do."

"I could haunt the tavern. That would hurt their business."

"I think that's a great idea. I could go invisible and spill beer everywhere."

"Let's start tomorrow night!"

"We're onto something," I say, laughing.

The sun rises on a crisp, clear winter day. I eat some venison while Shadow chews on a bone. I soak my feet in the cold quarry lake, calming my mind until the ache from the cold forces me out.

I decide to experiment. I head up the road to the castle and slip on the ring. Nothing happens. I take it off, go halfway back to the lodge, and try again. A tingling spreads through my body—I'm partially visible. As I move closer, I become fully visible again. The tingling intensifies into a strong, not uncomfortable, but unnerving vibration.

I remove my tunic and shirt and step forward. My limbs elongate, my chest deepens, my lower face starts to extend. I let the changes finish. A red mist clouds the edges of my vision.

"Pierre! I told you how dangerous this is," says Emelda, suddenly in front of me.

I back away until the effects subside and I can remove the ring.

"Proximity testing. I wish I'd thought of that earlier."

I smile at her as I dress. "Do you remember anything from combining the three pieces?"

"It was a long time ago, but I remember strange, flying dreams."

"I think the problem is a lack of control and awareness when the three are active."

"You could be right. But there's no safe way to find out. Look at what happened to me."

"I agree. I don't think anything good will come of it."

Later that afternoon, I finish cleaning the dried deer pelts and burn the remains by the lake. I toss a stick into the water for Shadow, who dives in and retrieves it, tail wagging, water spraying as he shakes himself dry—soaking me in the process.

Just then, Ivan comes puffing up the road, the duffel bag slung over his shoulder.

"Ivan, I didn't think I'd see you again."

"I brought your things—and some food from Dorris," he says stiffly.

"Do you want to take the crossbow back?"

"Yes, I will." He relaxes a bit. I gather the crossbow and bolts and hand them to him.

"Thank you, Ivan—for everything."

He sighs, then hugs me in a crushing embrace. "I can't stay angry with you, Pierre. Stop by the market square and say hello next time you're in town."

"I will. Maybe I'll bring some truffles."

Ivan snorts a laugh. Then, glancing at the fire, he adds, "You're making a lot of smoke. There's a new peacekeeper in town. Fresh out of the army—and looking for trouble."

"I'll do my best to stay out of his way."

"That's what worries me," he chuckles, walking off.

As dusk falls, I head to the Falandor Tavern. I hide the dagger at the base of the fountain in the town square and step inside. I take a corner table with a good view of the bar and door. The place begins to fill—farmers, laborers, merchants, canal workers—relaxing after a long day. Laughter and chatter grow louder.

I slip the ring on and vanish.

I approach two farmers in a heated but friendly argument and nudge one's elbow. Beer splashes on the other's shirt.

"Hey! Watch yourself!"

"I got bumped," says the first, glancing behind him.

I nudge the second man. More beer spills. A hard fist flies and the fight begins. I keep bumping people until a full brawl erupts.

Bartholomew Glamier stands behind the bar, sneering as he watches the chaos. His thin, anxious wife wrings her hands behind him.

Right on cue, Emelda sweeps into the crowd, arms raised, dancing among the combatants. The fighting freezes, a single breath of terrified silence—and then, panic. Everyone rushes for the door, stumbling, shoving, screaming.

I slip off the ring and follow the last of them out, leaving a broken, beer-soaked mess behind.

As the square empties, I return to the fountain to retrieve the dagger.

"Is this what you're looking for?"

I didn't see him there. Squint is holding the dagger, flanked by his two friends.

I straighten and say nothing.

"Cat got your tongue?" sneers Squint. His friends chuckle, moving to surround me.

"You know, scars give a man character," he says, flicking the blade.

"You don't have to do this, Squint. You can walk away."

"Or what? What are you going to do?"

"You don't want to know."

"Oh, but I do. Share your little secret, Pierre." His friends echo him.

"I don't think you'd like it."

"I think you're bluffing. You don't want me to cut you." He grins.

"No, please don't."

"Grab him, boys."

I slip the ring onto my finger.

A boiling eruption rises in my gut. Pain, rage, fear—all of it explodes. My body swells. My clothes tear at the seams. My mouth stretches into a maw of fangs. Red mist fills my vision. My hands are claws.

I roar.

Squint stands frozen, the dagger dropped. His scream pierces the night.

I become a nightmare.

I slash. I tear. I rip him apart in a frenzy of rage and blood.

Blood everywhere.

Blood covers the ground.

Slippery, red blood.

So much blood.

I run.

Fast.

The mist lifts.

Vision clears.

Faster still.

I reach the forest, slowing.

Shrinking.

Walking.

Shaking.
Covered in sticky blood.
My body screams in pain.
I collapse, roll into a pile of leaves—and pass out.

Chapter Twelve The Promise

First light prods me awake. My head throbs with pain, and my eyes sting as I try to open them. I can hear Emelda calling me and realize I'm still invisible. I slip the ring off, and a wet tongue begins lapping the side of my face—again and again.

"Stop it, Shadow," I say, sitting up. I look down at myself—my clothes hang in blood-soaked strips, and leaves cling to me where the blood is drying.

"Get up and move!" Emelda shouts, panic in her voice. "They are coming to find you!"

I get to my feet and stumble back to the crossroads, then start up the hill, peeling off my ruined tunic as I walk. At the hairpin bend, I strip off the rest of my clothes, climb down, and step under the waterfall. The water is freezing cold, but the blood washes away. I keep scrubbing until I'm clean.

Climbing back to the road, I gather the pile of bloody rags and head up to the lodge. I open the duffel bag, set aside the food Dorris packed, dress in my old clothes, and repack the food. With my bag slung over one shoulder, the deer skins over the other, and Shadow beside me, I make my way to the ruined castle.

Digging through the ruined tunic, I find the ring and pocket it. I throw the bloody rags and skins into the castle's privy and sit to rest. I pull out the food and notice something deeper in the bag—a neatly folded piece of paper. I unfold it and stare at the words.

"What does it say?" asks Emelda.

"No idea. I can't read," I admit, embarrassment reddening my cheeks.

"Allow me," she says.

Dear Pierre,

Ivan has told me about the magical things that have come into your possession.

It makes no difference to how I feel about you.

You will always be like a son to me, and you are welcome in our home anytime.

We want only the best for you and hope your fortunes improve in the coming days.

With much love,

From your friends,

Dorris and Ivan

"Thanks for reading that to me, Emelda. I wish I could read."

"You hang on to that letter. With practice, you'll be able to read it someday."

We hear men's voices in the quarry below. I get to my feet and say, "I have to go, but I'll be back. I promise. And when I do, the Glamier family will get what they deserve."

"I will be glad of that, Pierre. Farewell."

I quickly head off down the main ridgeline, following an old logging trail through the pine trees. Shadow stays close behind. We walk swiftly, passing Falandor Town on the plain below. When the sun is high, we stop to rest, and I unwrap the smoked pork from Dorris. I'm deeply grateful for her kindness. I promise myself that, somehow, I will return that kindness to her and Ivan. I give Shadow a few chunks of meat, which he swallows as if he's never eaten in his life.

After a few more hours of walking, the ridge flattens into a wide, gently sloping plateau covered with large oak trees. Shadow, nose down, zigzags along and finds a cluster of truffles. I pick them up, put them in my bag, and we keep moving.

Eventually, we reach a wide road heading south and follow it. Soon, we come to a town similar to Falandor. We pass through it, find the canal, and continue walking along its edge. The canal runs out from the town through open farmland, where farmers are harvesting cabbages in the fields.

Up ahead is a canal lock. We take the higher road to bypass the busy area, where loaded barges, horses, and men wait for the water to rise or fall. I can't afford to be seen—my current status makes me a wanted man.

By late afternoon, the next town comes into view. We stop by a stone bridge, climb down the embankment beside the canal, and set up camp. I find windfallen branches and drag them under the bridge. Further along, I spot a rabbit warren. I slip on the ring and become invisible again. Quietly, I grab an unsuspecting rabbit and cut its throat. I get two more and give one to Shadow.

With a fire going and rabbit roasting, I pull out my sewing kit and stitch a hidden pouch inside the front of my trousers—big enough to conceal the ring and amulet. When we reach the city, there will be plenty of pickpockets, and these magical items are irreplaceable.

Rain begins to fall—light at first, then a heavy downpour that lasts well into the night.

By morning, the rain has eased to a light shower as we approach the town. It's much bigger than Falandor, with a wide main road running through its center. Shadow waits outside while I step into a tavern, hoping to sell the truffles we found yesterday.

At the bar, I ask to speak with the chef. A moment later, a large, round man appears.

"What can I do for you, young man?" he asks.

I place the truffles on the counter. His eyebrows lift slightly as he picks one up and sniffs it.

"Hmm. You selling?"

"I am. For a fair price."

"One gold dollar, alright?"

I hide my reaction and nod. He hands me a coin from a drawer, nods again, and takes the truffles to the kitchen.

As I leave the tavern, I think about how much money Ivan made and regret not making a deal with him. Maybe when I return, I'll see if he's still interested.

As we walk, the canal widens, and the roads on either side grow broader. An hour later, we reach a wide, deep river. Barges are towed along by teams of horses. A high, broad bridge spans the water, its massive pylons sunk into the riverbed. I stop and scratch behind Shadow's ear. He looks up at me, smiling, tail wagging.

Looking down the river, I see a gray smoky cloud hanging over the horizon. The road is bustling with horse-drawn wagons, buggies, lone riders, and people on foot—all heading toward the city.

We pass rows of warehouses. I hear a steady thump, thump, thump and see gray smoke rising from a chimney. What I first thought were cliffs beside the river turn out to be towering buildings with smoke stacks rising above them. Thick smoke belches out, adding to the pollution already hanging in the air.

The noise and smell are overwhelming—but more overwhelming is the sheer number of people coming and going, queuing, handling horses, and shoveling coal from the long lines of barges.

Chapter Thirteen The Fortune Teller

We cross the river using a floating wooden bridge into a quieter area, where buildings are under construction. Further along, a canvas town of tents has been erected—temporary shelters for the flood of migrant workers arriving in the city. We pass by the tents and continue along the river. Huge sailing ships are tied to the wharfs, loading and unloading all sorts of materials. The air smells different now—fresh and salty.

We climb a sand hill, and suddenly the wide blue sea opens up before us. White waves break on a long sandy beach. The sight, sound, and scent of it all take my breath away. I take off my boots and walk down to the edge of the water. Lost in the beauty of the place, I stroll along the shore. Shadow splashes beside me, trying to bite the waves.

At the far end of the beach, I spot someone walking toward us. As they get closer, I see it's a woman dressed in loose white clothing. Shadow runs to her, tail wagging high. She bends to pat him affectionately.

She straightens to face me. She's older than me, with loose, black wavy hair falling around her shoulders. Her eyes are black and sparkling. A strong jawline, big white teeth, and a hooked nose define her striking face. Her brown skin glows with health.

She places a hand on her chest and says, "Valeria," in a thick foreign accent, then gestures toward me.

"Pierre," I reply, copying the gesture.

"You have nice dog," she says, patting Shadow again.

"Shadow," I say, but she just looks blankly at me and continues patting him.

"You swim?" she asks. Then, with two quick motions, she drops her clothes and walks naked into the water.

I fumble out of my clothes and follow. The waves splash cool and sharp against my body—it feels wonderful. Neck-deep in the surf, I glance around and realize she's gone. Suddenly, something tugs my feet from under me, and I go under. I surface coughing and sputtering, and see her laughing at me. She swims away, then flips onto her back, floating and smiling.

Her body is strong and muscular—almost like a man's—but her curves are undeniably feminine. She moves behind me, gently pulls my shoulders back until I'm floating, then supports my back with her hands, looking me over like I'm a meal she's about to eat. Then she kisses me.

I kiss her back. Together, we crash through the breaking waves and tumble onto the beach. She pushes me onto my back, straddles me, cups my face in her hands, and kisses me again. Suddenly, I'm inside her. She grinds her hips, taking control, my hands on her waist.

She runs her fingers through her wet hair, over her breasts, down her stomach, continuing to move atop me. Then she gasps, moans, and begins to tremble violently as she orgasms.

I'm on the edge of climax when she abruptly stands, smiling and wagging her finger. She gets dressed and walks away along the beach, glancing back to beckon me forward. I hurry to dress and catch up. Shadow trots beside me, his wet fur glistening in the sun.

We leave the beach and head into the sandhills, following a rough trail through tussock grass and tough coastal shrubs. Eventually, we reach a small grassy meadow where an ornate wagon is parked. A large horse grazes nearby.

A huge man steps out from behind the wagon, carrying an armful of firewood and an axe. He has long braided red hair and a thick beard. Tattoos decorate his cheekbones, and his blue eyes scowl at me from under heavy brows.

"Hola, Chino," he grunts, dropping the wood beside the fire and swinging the axe into a chopping block with one hand.

"I find them on beach," Valeria says, pointing to Shadow and me. Then she gestures to the man. "Carlos."

"Hello, Carlos," I say.

He grunts dismissively and begins preparing food at a bench beside the wagon.

"Come," says Valeria, leading me around to a small black canvas room attached to the side of the wagon.

Inside is a small table with stools on either side. She lights a candle and we sit, facing one another. She takes my hand, traces the scar Glamier gave me with a finger, tuts softly, then turns my palm over and studies it. Her eyebrows rise, and she nods.

She spreads out a deck of strange cards and invites me to choose. I select a few, and she turns them face-up, laying them in a pattern. The illustrations remind me of stained-glass windows in churches—but twisted, filled with mayhem and madness.

Suddenly, Valeria sits upright, eyes narrowing until only her black irises are visible. She looks almost inhuman, and I feel a chill.

"You grease the age and make the change to come," she says cryptically.

Then she slumps forward, rubbing her eyes.

"Enough!" she snaps, and pushes me out of the booth.

We return to the fire, where Carlos is cooking. I don't understand what she meant, and I feel uneasy around them, but the sun is setting, so I stay. Carlos serves three bowls of spicy stew. I thank him. He grunts. We eat in silence. The food is delicious—hot and bold.

Afterward, Carlos gets up, reaches for Valeria, and pulls her into a rough embrace. She responds in kind, and together they climb into the wagon. A moment later, I hear rhythmic thumping, moaning, and grunting from inside—sounds that go on well into the night.

I curl up beside the fire with Shadow and fall asleep.

Loud voices wake me before dawn. Carlos and Valeria are arguing in their language. I don't understand, so I get up and prepare to leave.

"Hey, Chino! You come work," Carlos calls, gesturing for me to follow.

I need money, so I tell Shadow to stay and follow him into the grey dawn.

We cross a low wooden bridge toward the noisy, clattering factory buildings. Coal barges are moored at a floating dock, and horses with single-axle wagons wait to be loaded.

I follow Carlos onto the dock. A man on a coal barge waves us aboard.

"I pay you when empty," he says, tossing us each a shovel.

Carlos starts shoveling with graceful efficiency—two scoops to every one of mine. I grunt and sweat, trying to keep up. We take a short break while another wagon rolls in, then start again. Carlos sneers, shaking his head at my struggle. I feel hopelessly inadequate, but I won't give up. My arms and shoulders ache, and my old clothes begin falling apart.

By midday, the barge is empty. The man pays us. Carlos leaps to the next barge like he's just getting started. I point to my ripped clothes and ask a wagon driver where I can find shops. He gives me directions.

I follow a wide street lined with shops—some selling food, herbs, and spices, others offering furniture and bedding. I find a clothing store, buy black canvas trousers, boots, and a shirt, then return to the dock with half my money spent.

Carlos is still shoveling, nearly halfway through the next barge. I feel nervous around him—unsafe—so I decide to collect Shadow and leave while I still can.

I stop by the tent town to ask about accommodation and realize I'll need more money to stay. Mid-afternoon, I return to the meadow.

Shadow greets me eagerly. As I approach the wagon, I see Valeria dressed in tight leather pants, knee-high boots, and a solid leather vest. A hunting knife hangs from her hip. A pig is roasting over the fire.

"Good dog," she says, pointing to Shadow, who wags his tail, tongue lolling happily. I notice stab wounds on the pig—evidence of Valeria's deadly skills.

"I need to go, Valeria," I say, almost apologetically. "Carlos hates me."

"Ha! You not worry about him," she laughs.

Just then, Carlos strides into the camp, fury on his face.

"Lazy Chino," he snarls, pointing at me.

Valeria steps in front of him, waving her arms and shouting. He swings a hand at her, but she ducks, knees him in the groin, and shoves him backward. He crumples, groaning on the ground in a fetal position.

I stand frozen, mouth open in shock.

Valeria turns on me, red-hot anger on her face. "What you stare at, eh?"

Chapter Fourteen Loss and Poison

The food is served and eaten in silence. Carlos is sulking, childishly stealing nasty glances at me whenever Valeria isn't watching.

I'm so exhausted from the day that I fall asleep by the fire as soon as I finish eating.

I dream of a forge in a desert. A black man is hammering a blade into shape, singing curses over it, and quenching the red-hot steel in a bath of blood. A wizard casts spells into the blade, with Emelda at his side. Then the desert again—battle raging across the sands, the dagger soaked in blood, taken by armored men on horseback. Back to Emelda and the wizard, weaving more magic into the blade.

"It works," says Emelda.

"It has blood magic in it. That's why it works," says the wizard.

The forge again. Emelda again. Around and around it goes. I sleep on and on.

Bright sunlight pierces my groggy consciousness. I groan and roll over, trying to cling to sleep, but the heat and light prod me awake. I give in and open my eyes.

As I sit up, I forget where I am. The wagon house has gone —the horse, Valeria, and Carlos are gone. Most of the day is gone too. My coin pouch has been cut, and I have no money. I stand, unsteady on my feet, and look around. They must have poisoned me.

"Shadow!" I call out.

"Shadow!" Still nothing.

Thankfully, I'm still wearing my old trousers under my new ones, and Valeria and Carlos didn't find the ring and amulet in my hidden pocket. I put on the amulet and concentrate on Shadow. I can feel him—but he's not close. I will find him again. I'm sure of it.

I still have my bag with a few things in it, so I shoulder it and walk into the city.

Crossing the bridge, I approach the factory buildings and ask for work.

"Night shift starts in an hour," says the foreman. "Come back then."

I find a pawn shop and borrow some money. Leaving the ring behind makes me nervous, but I have to eat.

On a main street corner, I spot a large tavern. I go in, get a meal, and make it back to the factory with plenty of time before night shift begins.

The job involves shoveling coal into a furnace. The building has two large open doorways at the front. I peek inside and see two men shoveling coal from a pile into the glowing fire of the furnace. Behind the furnace, a series of levers and wheels moves in time with the steady thumping of the steam engine. Another man stands at the controls, adjusting handles and watching a round glass window attached to the machinery.

A loud whistle blows. The men put down their tools, walk over to the wall between the two doorways, drink and wash from a water barrel, then head out.

The foreman enters with another man—about my age and build. He points to the shovels and furnace.

"Work," is his only instruction.

Together, we shovel coal into the fire until the floor is clean. We grab drinks from the barrel and wash the soot from our faces.

"Pierre," I say.

"Jack," says the man. We shake hands briefly.

A horse and buggy swing into the space between us and the furnace. The driver jumps down, grabs the shovel from me, and says, "Wedge it in here and there," pointing to notches under the wagon tray. We slot our shovels in, pull down, and the tray tilts. Coal spills into a pile on the floor. The tray resets, and the wagon rolls out the other side.

We keep shoveling until the pile is gone, take a water break, then start again.

I'm getting into the rhythm of the work now. Before I know it, daylight streams through the big doors, and the whistle blows for the shift change.

The morning is clear and bright. The foreman pays me, and we agree on the same arrangement for tonight.

I return to the pawn shop and hand over my slip of paper, asking for the ring back. A small, thin man with a bald pate and a long nose peers at me through half-moon spectacles. He produces a ring—but it's not mine.

"That's not my ring."

"Oh, terribly sorry, sir. My mistake." He ducks back under the counter and returns with the correct ring. I let out a sigh, realizing I've been holding my breath.

"Would you like to sell this ring? I could offer you a very good deal."

"No. It's not for sale."

"Oh well, I'll just try it on before you buy it back."

Before I can stop him, he slips the ring on—and vanishes.

I hear choking, gasping. A moment later, he reappears, eyes wide and face pale. Pulling the ring off and slamming it onto the counter, shaking.

"If you ever tell anyone about this," I say, "I'll come back and choke the life out of you."

"I won't! I promise!" he pleads.

I glare at him, snatch the ring, and stride out of the shop—forgetting to give him the money.

I wander along the busy street, weaving through crowds of people. Horses and wagons travel both ways, and there's no room to stop without risking being knocked down.

I find another tavern and eat my fill, but Shadow's on my mind. I decide to search for him now, before I sleep or do anything else.

Turning into a quieter side street, I put on the amulet and try to sense him again. I can still feel his presence—faint, almost hidden from the amulet's magic.

A dog barks. It sounds like Shadow. I head in the direction of the sound. As it grows louder, I see the dog and think it might be him.

I get closer—but the dog snarls, barking and snapping from the end of its chain. I send calm thoughts to the frightened animal. Slowly, it settles enough to let me pass.

The city is crowded, the buildings tall and packed tightly together. The amulet doesn't work as well here as it did in the quiet forest and the town of Falandor.

The day is mild and calm, so I head to the sand hills to catch some sleep.

Things feel like they're starting to improve—but without my dog, it's like eating food with no flavor. I decide to search for him every day after work and drift off to sleep with that thought in my mind.

A chilly sea breeze wakes me at dusk as darkness creeps along the coast. I make my way back to the noisy clatter and slap and thump of the city I'm starting to get used to.

Finding a tavern serving fresh food, I eat. After another meal, I wait for night shift to begin.

Chapter Fifteen Eli

Jack, my workmate, arrives just after me, and the whistle blows for the shift change. I strike up a conversation during the break.

"What brings you to the city, Jack?"

"I was a farm worker, three days up the river from here. More and more people were leaving town, so I came to see it for myself," he says, almost embarrassed to be one of the many thousands who've come here for similar reasons.

Another cart is towed into position. We unload it and swing into work with a steady rhythm. My muscles are becoming accustomed to the demands I place on them, but the constant sweating from the heat is still a challenge.

A loud, sudden cracking and hissing sound rises above the ambient noise as a shower of hot water and steam sprays from Jack's side of the boiler, hitting his body and knocking him flat. He lies on the ground, screaming and writhing in pain. The foreman comes running, followed by another man with a bucket of water. He douses Jack in an attempt to cool the heat that's blistering his skin.

A gurney arrives. Jack is lifted onto it and taken away. His cries fade into the surrounding noise.

I freeze, staring into space, as I remember watching my father being crushed between the huge gear wheels of the flour mill.

"You alright, lad?" says the foreman, snapping me back to the moment.

"Not really, but I can still work, if you need me to."

"Good. Follow me." He leads me to another building with a furnace like the one I just left. Feeling numb and confused from what I just saw, I pick up the shovel and keep working.

The last scrap of coal has been scraped from the floor. I take some water and wash my face. A warm, rich voice lures me back to the present.

"Hello, my name is Eli," says a black man with white hair and a broad smile, offering me his hand.

"Hello Eli, I'm Pierre," I say, shaking hands with him.

"Oh, Pierre. Pleased to meet you," he replies, his smile widening and lighting up his lined face.

As we work, I notice the skin on his back. He has a crisscross array of scars from his lower back up over his shoulders. He catches me looking, smiles, and winks, as if his scars are a badge of honour. But they are the scars of a slave—one beaten and abused, but not broken.

The first light of day has crept through the large open doorways without me noticing, and the whistle signals the end of the shift.

"Pierre, would you like to come and share a meal with me?" asks Eli.

I accept, and he leads me to a tavern on a quiet street corner in an old part of the city. We sit down to eat, and Eli starts talking.

"Pierre, this is my favourite part of the city. My master used to bring me here. We would eat and drink. He would read to me and teach me how to read."

"Were you his slave?"

Eli laughs. "He pretended I was his slave, to stop people from judging us, but really we were just very good friends."

"How did you meet him?"

"I was a slave before I met him. Five other slaves and I were unloading a barge stacked too high with timber, and it capsized. We were trapped underwater. I found a pocket of air between the boards while the others drowned. As another group of slaves pulled the timber out, I drowned too. We were hauled from the river and thrown onto a cart, bound for the cemetery. As the cart jolted along the road, I came back to life. At the cemetery, Doctor Pierre was checking for survivors. He found that I was alive—barely. He took me to his surgery and nursed me back to health. That was the luckiest day of my life."

"Doctor Pierre?"

"Yes, you have the same name."

"Is he still alive?"

Eli takes a deep breath, choking back tears. "Almost two years ago, he died. His brother hated our friendship and turned me out with nothing but the clothes on my back. It broke my heart losing him like that."

"I lost my mother and father around the same time. I know how it feels."

"Well, enough said. What about you, Pierre? Any plans for this morning?"

"I need to find my dog. If I keep looking, I'm sure I'll find him. Then I'm going back to the countryside."

"Well, good luck. I hope to see you at work this evening."

"I'll be there."

I wander the streets and back alleyways, checking every bark, yelp, and whine. As I round a corner, a large hand clamps onto my shoulder. I turn and come face to face with Robert, the peacekeeper from Falandor.

"I remember you. There was a nasty murder there not long ago. Know anything about it?"

"No, sir. I haven't been to Falandor since I saw you last," I lie.

"Hmm. Not sure I believe that. The local priest was found dead the day you were meant to surrender your feral dog. How do you explain that?"

"I went back to Mill Town. It had nothing to do with me."

"I don't have enough evidence to arrest you. But here's some advice—if I catch you doing anything wrong, I'll lock you up so fast your head will spin."

I say nothing, just nod and walk away—fighting the urge to run.

The tent city is a safe haven. For a small cost, I can rent a tent during the day. I sew a hidden pocket into my trousers for the amulet and the ring. I repair my coin pouch and attach it the same way. In my duffel bag, I find the letter from Dorris and wonder how they're faring in these changing times. I want to read it, but I don't know where to start or how to make sense of the squiggly lines.

Sleep claims me. I wake to dusk stretching down the roof of my tent, ushering in the cool of evening.

I find a hot meal at a tavern, then return to the noisy workplace I'm starting to enjoy.

It's good to see Eli again. He's warm and friendly, but it's hard to trust anyone after Valeria and Carlos's betrayal. Still, we work calmly together, sharing pleasantries during breaks.

The whistle blows. Eli invites me to breakfast again, and we return to the quiet tavern.

Two plates of bacon, eggs, and bread land softly on the table, followed by steaming coffee.

"Eli, I need a haircut and shave. Know a good barber?"

"I do. I could use a trim myself—we'll go together."

"You said you can read. I have a letter from my friends in Falandor. Could you read it to me?"

I hand him the letter from Dorris. He squints, reads silently, then clears his throat and reads aloud in his deep, rich voice. He sets the letter down and looks at me without speaking.

"Thanks, Eli. It's good to hear that again. I miss them."

"They clearly love you like a son. It's rare to meet people like that. What are the magical things mentioned in the letter?"

I was hoping he wouldn't ask. "I'll show you when the time is right—not here, not now."

"Alright, suit yourself. You know, if you want to learn to read, I could teach you."

"I'd like that. Very much."

"Well, we start with the first letter of your name and go from there."

We leave the tavern. Eli points to the letter 'Pee' on street signs and shop windows. As we walk, he has me say words starting with it. We arrive at the barbershop and sit down.

In the mirror, I hardly recognize myself. My beard is scraggly, my hair wild. My dark eyes look hard and flinty, my cheekbones sharp. The boy is gone from my face, though he still lives in my mind.

"Eli, can I ask you something?"

"Of course, Pierre. Anything."

"When you were a slave... was life harder than it is now?"

"In some ways, yes. But we were given food, clothes, and a place to sleep. We had no money and were owned."

"That sounds awful. Being someone's property."

"It was. But you know, I'm still a slave. I spend all my money on food, clothes, and rent. If I stop working, I'll starve or freeze. It's the same coin—just different sides."

"So I'm a slave too."

"Yes, you are. So is everyone else—unless they're clever enough to run a business and get others to work for them. They took off the old shackles and gave us new ones."

He pulls out a coin, holds it up. "These are the new shackles."

The barber grunts disapproval and gets to work. He shaves my beard, trims my hair into a neat ponytail. In the mirror, I see someone new. Someone the peacekeeper might not recognize.

Eli joins me in the continued search for Shadow. As we pass old stone houses on a hill, Eli pauses.

"Sorry, Pierre. My breathing's been bad since I drowned."

"Take your time," I say.

We're near a large cemetery.

"Would you mind visiting Doctor Pierre's grave?"

"Let's do it."

As we walk, the reading lesson continues. Some letters are becoming familiar. We stop at the headstone. Eli lets a tear fall down his cheek. I think of my parents' graves—simple wooden crosses.

We take a different route back to the river, following every bark and growl. But no sign of Shadow.

"I'm going back to the tent city for some sleep," I say.

"You could get a room where I stay."

I look at him. I can't find a reason not to trust him. "That would be good. Lead the way."

We return to the old part of the city and enter a tall, narrow building. In the foyer, a fat man snores behind the counter.

Eli knocks a few times. The man wakes, stretches. "The usual room?"

"Yes, please," Eli says, handing over coins for a key.

"I'd like a room too," I say.

"Get lost. We're full," the man says with a toad-like stare. "Not just anyone can stay here."

I turn to leave. Eli stops me.

"I can vouch for him."

The man grunts, scratches his neck. "Alright then."

I trade coins for a key. Eli helps me find my room. It's small and bare—but clean. A bed. A window. A lockable door.

"Thanks, Eli. See you tonight."

"Sleep well."

I'm back in the quarry lodge. Andre, the priest, points a crossbow at Shadow. I step in front of him—he shoots me. I start falling and falling...

I wake sweating. Later, a knock at the door. It's nearly dark.

"Let's go," Eli says.

We return to the tavern, then to work, then continue searching for Shadow. Days pass. Then weeks. Then months. Summer arrives.

"I was thinking, Eli—maybe I should look for Shadow at night. What do you think?"

"You could take a few nights off. I'll come with you."

My reading has improved. I recognize shop signs, street names. I even walk past Robert unnoticed. We tell the foreman we'll be away for a few nights. The rest of the day is spent browsing shops and practicing reading.

At night, the city transforms. Oil lamps flicker on corners. Music and laughter spill from taverns.

Down a familiar narrow street, we spot him—Shadow. Chained in an alley, growling.

A large man with a cane and a limp steps out. "Hey—you two. Keep walking."

"That's my dog."

"No, he's mine. Bought him from gypsies. Cost me a fortune."

"They stole him from me."

"That's enough. You and your slave can bugger off unless you want to taste my whip."

He unhooks it from his belt, lets it uncoil. Eli steps forward, kicks the cane out from under him. The man crashes down, cursing.

"I'll whip you good, filthy slave!" he snarls, flicking the whip.

Eli catches it. The man punches him, trying to get up. Eli loops the whip around his neck and pulls tight, knee in his back.

"These scars—you gave them to me. I've dreamed of this moment."

The man claws at the whip, choking. He jerks, kicks—then goes limp. Eli lets go, breath ragged.

I untie Shadow. He's thin, ribs showing—but alive.

"Come with us, Eli. You can't stay here."

"You're right. I feel good having my revenge. But I don't want to die in a jail cell."

On the way out of the city, we stop at a tavern. Three bowls of stew. Shadow devours his. Then looks at me, tail tapping.

We share a long look, like we've done many times before.

Chapter Sixteen The Roaring Silence

A grey dawn illuminates the overcast sky as we approach the large bridge spanning the river. We stop in the middle for a few minutes, gazing at the smoky horizon.

"You know what, Eli? I could take or leave that city. But I have to say—I've never learned so much so quickly before. Thank you for teaching me. I appreciate it very much."

"Well, you're most welcome, my friend. It's been a pleasure teaching you. I've never been this far from the city before," he says, a look of wonder and excitement flashing across his lined face.

We wander into the first town across the river, and I purchase some cooking supplies, two tin mugs, and coffee. Walking along the wide canal, I feel like I can finally breathe again after months of smoke and dust in my throat. I notice Eli coughing more often than usual, and he seems short of breath.

We reach the large stone bridge where Shadow and I spent the night before our final day's journey to the city—just as it starts to rain.

"I stopped here to shelter from the rain on my way to the city... and again, it's raining." Gathering firewood from the roadside, I notice an abandoned farmhouse not far ahead. "Change of plan, Eli. Follow me."

We hurry and reach the house before getting too wet. I push open the back door, and we step into an old kitchen, not unlike Dorris and Ivan's room. I light a fire and bring in more wood until we've got a cheerful blaze going.

Eli starts laughing. "This is wonderful, Pierre. We can enjoy a fire without swinging a shovel!"

I smile as I watch him. I understand how hard his life has been, and yet he can still appreciate simple pleasures. It's a testament to the strength of spirit in this man. He's refused to be embittered by the harsh, brutal realities of life. I intend to carry that inspiration with me into my own future.

Shadow curls up by the fire, his chin resting on his paws, watching every move I make. I set an iron pot over the flames, fill it with water, and begin preparing vegetables for a stew. When I drop them in, a splash hits the scar on the back of my hand—the one Glamier gave me. I wince and shake my hand.

"You never told me how you got that scar," says Eli, his tone gently curious.

I sigh and tell him how I was arrested—and how Glamier dragged the blade through my skin.

"So, what will you do about this Glamier—to set things right?"

"I want to kill him," I say, rubbing my face with my hands and pressing them together in front of my mouth like a prayer.

"There are better ways to get revenge—ways that don't risk your own life."

"I made a promise to someone. A promise I have to keep. So he has to die."

"What if he's caught in the act and executed?"

I look at Eli and nod, as a plan begins to form in my mind.

"I want to show you the magical things I have. Remember the letter?"

"Yes, I haven't forgotten."

I place the amulet and the ring on the table. Eli stares at them in amazement, then looks at me.

"I know they're pretty things, but their true value is in what they do." I put on the amulet, slide the ring onto my finger—and vanish.

Eli's mouth drops open, his eyes bulging wide. I remove the ring and reappear. He stares, lost for words.

"How..." He starts laughing, then his laughter turns to coughing, tears streaming down his face as he gathers himself. "That's amazing, Pierre. And you've had these things all along? Since I've known you?"

"I have. You can imagine the kind of trouble I'd be in if people found out."

"Yes, indeed. People would kill to have magic like that. But how did you get them?" His face lights up with curiosity.

I tell him most of the story—but say nothing about Emelda. Whether he believes in ghosts or not, I don't think it's wise to bring her up.

I serve three helpings of stew, and we eat our fill as a grey mist creeps across the countryside in the fading light. The rain has stopped, and the silence surrounding us seems unreal to Eli.

"It's so quiet here. I never knew it could be like this. The city always has noise—even before the steam machines and factories, it was never this quiet."

"Do you like the silence?"

"I can't say that I like it. It's so strange—like nothing I've ever experienced."

I fetch another armful of firewood from the backyard and stoke the fire until it crackles happily in the hearth.

Eli and I sit in silence, watching the flames. The fire hisses and snaps loudly in the stillness of the night. Shadow starts snoring. We glance at each other and smile, warmed by the comfort of a contented dog whose neglect and confinement ended less than a day ago.

"I think we should get some sleep. We've got a long walk ahead of us tomorrow," I say.

We find some bedding and sleep on the floor by the fire.

Scratching and whining wake me. It's still dark. Shadow is desperate to get outside. I open the door and step into the night. I watch my dog strain to relieve himself—his body still adjusting after so long without food. When he finishes, he wipes his back feet on the wet grass and swaggers up to me, tail swishing.

I crouch and pull him into my arms, giving him a gentle hug and stroking his bony frame. I think about hunting another deer when we return. I get up, scratching him behind the ears. The first pale hint of dawn glows in the eastern sky. I go inside to start the fire.

Some kindling and a steady breath bring the coals back to life. I pile on more wood, and warm firelight floods the room.

"Hey, Eli, wake up."

No response.

I crouch beside him and give him a shake. "Wake up, Eli." Still nothing. I touch his face—he's cold. I lean in, listening for breath. Nothing. I press my ear to his chest. No heartbeat.

Oh no. Eli. No, no, no.

Panic floods me as I try to shake him awake, but he's gone. In the silence of the night, he slipped peacefully and quietly out of this life. He went home.

Tears well up, and I weep for my friend.

As the sun rises, I find tools in the farmhouse shed. On the edge of the abandoned field, I bury my friend—my teacher—someone who showed me more kindness and respect than I thought possible. Life was harsh and cruel to him, yet he still had room in his heart for love and compassion. If the world had more people like him, it would be a better place.

I don't mark his grave, remembering the barbaric statue of the tortured man nailed to a cross. I walk away, believing this is what Eli would have wanted.

Chapter Seventeen A Serving of Revenge

Shadow and I follow the winding path of the canal for the rest of the day. We find a quiet place along the way, and using the ring and amulet, I catch and skin four rabbits. We make camp under a huge willow tree by the water and roast two of our kills over a small fire. Shadow crunches and chews his way through his two rabbits while I enjoy the roasted meat. We sleep together by the fire and wake at sunrise.

Falandor is quiet as we walk along the canal path. I pause, staring at the once-bustling market square, now empty. We continue on and eventually reach the crossroads. Climbing the familiar road to the lodge feels easier than before. I'm stronger and heavier than I've ever been, but the choking smoke and dust seem to have settled in my chest. By the time we reach the lodge, I'm puffing and gasping for air.

I open the door and step inside. Everything is just as I left it. I gather some firewood, sharpen my new hunting knife, put on the ring and amulet, and head out to hunt.

I make my kill on the saddle and carry the deer back to the lodge. The butcher frame is still where I left it, so I put it to use once more. I carve raw meat from a hind leg and give Shadow the bone. He trots to the edge of the quarry lake and strips it clean.

Dusk settles on a clear summer evening. I light the fire and start smoking the meat. I roast a few choice cuts. We sit by the fire, full and satisfied.

"Well, this is cozy!" says Emelda in her usual manner.

"I've been expecting you," I reply, not giving her the satisfaction of startling me like before.

"Nice to see you too," she says, watching the fire thoughtfully. "Back here to keep your promise, I hope."

"Of course. It's time to put your despicable family out of business—permanently."

"Emelda, I want to ask you something about that dagger," I say, making sure I have her attention.

"Oh, are you still harping on about that old thing? Alright, what is it?"

"Did the blade have any curses or magic in it before you and your wizard enchanted it?"

"Yes, it had an old blood curse. How did you know about that?"

"I dreamed it. I was poisoned and robbed."

"Well, well. You've had quite a time in the big city."

"Trust me, it wasn't much fun. Would you say the dagger is... bloodthirsty?"

"Oh yes. That night after we haunted the tavern, Squint only meant to scratch you—to scare you. If he had, he wouldn't have been able to stop. You'd be as dead as I am."

"When Glamier cut my hand, he wanted to keep going, but the peacekeeper stopped him."

"That peacekeeper helped you more than you think. I see where you're going with this, but whatever you do—don't get caught. You're worth ten of Roger Glamier and his cousin."

"I have a plan, Emelda. And if it works, your wish will come true."

Sleep claims Shadow and me—long and dreamless. Dawn greets our eyes with a grey, windy day. I cut up an old shirt, wrap a bundle of smoked meat in it, and stuff it into my duffel bag.

I tell Shadow to stay, knowing he'll be safe, and give him a meaty bone to chew on. With my bag over my shoulder and dressed in my best clothes, I take the familiar road down the hill. Before long, I'm knocking on the back door of the old stone cottage.

Ivan opens the door and stares at me blankly. "What do you want?"

"Ivan, it's me—Pierre."

It takes a moment to register.

"Pierre! Come in, come in. Dorris, we have company."

Dorris sees me and pulls me into a warm embrace.

"Pierre, it's so good to see you. You've changed so much, I hardly recognized you."

"I didn't," admits Ivan, giving my upper arm a squeeze and patting me on the shoulder.

We sit at the table, and I answer all their questions about the city and the work I did. I notice dark rings under their eyes and the drawn lines of worry on their faces. I take out my parcel of smoked venison and place it on the table. Tears fill Dorris's eyes as she thanks me.

"After you skipped town, things got worse here," says Ivan with a sigh. "I stopped making money, business dried up, and our savings went to rent. Glamier comes nearly every day with the peacekeeper, demanding money. Looks like he'll evict us soon."

"Well, he hasn't changed. Still as greedy as he is mean."

Ivan nods and brushes away a tear. I don't mention what I've planned. As soon as I can, I excuse myself and head toward town.

Passing the town lockup, I see a prison wagon parked out front—solid timber with bars for windows. As I walk past Glamier's house, he's standing on the footpath, arguing with the peacekeeper.

They glance at me briefly, showing no recognition, and return to their argument. I duck into a side street and position myself where I can watch. Together, they walk in the direction of Ivan and Dorris's home. I circle the block and enter the Glamier mansion from the back, taking the familiar route through the kitchen. I reach the display cabinet and steal the dagger.

Taking a deep breath, I slip the ring on and make it to the front gate before I run out of air.

At the empty mid-morning tavern, I step up to the bar. No one is there. I place the dagger on the counter and drape a cloth over it, leaving a small part of the blade visible. I'm about to leave when Bartholomew Glamier emerges from the kitchen.

"What's your pleasure, sir?" he asks, clearly desperate for a sale.

"Are you open for lunch today?" I ask.

"Yes, certainly. We have a small menu available."

"Thanks. I'll see you at midday."

"We look forward to seeing you then," he says, his round, pink face attempting a smile.

Across the square, I spot a boy pretending to sword fight with a stick.

"Want to earn a few coins running errands?" I ask.

"I would," he replies, grinning gap-toothed.

"Here's one copper now. Meet me by the canal and I'll give you the other."

I tell him what to do, and he runs into the tavern. A minute later, he's back at my side. I give him another copper.

"What are you playing at, mister?" he asks.

"Just a little joke. Want to be part of it?"

He nods enthusiastically.

We go to the street corner and wait for the fat tavern owner to come out of the Glamier mansion. As he passes, I whisper to the boy, "Did you see the dagger he was carrying?"

"No."

"He did have it. When Lord Glamier comes home, I want you to tell him you saw Bartholomew with it."

We don't wait long. Glamier and the peacekeeper come into view. The boy rushes to deliver the message, and the two men immediately head toward the tavern.

I give the boy more coins and follow them along the main street into the tavern. I order a beer, take a slurp, and spill some down the front of my tunic. I pull the cloth from the counter, revealing the dagger.

A loud, aggressive argument erupts between the cousins. Bartholomew comes from behind the bar, sleeves rolled up. Roger picks up the dagger and waves it in his face.

I slip the ring on, grab Glamier's wrist, and thrust the blade into his cousin's neck.

Dark red blood gushes between Bartholomew's thick fingers as he clutches his throat. Roger Glamier stands frozen, mouth agape, the dagger still in his hand.

Right on cue, his wife enters the tavern and screams in horror at the scene.

The peacekeeper says nothing. He plucks the dagger from Roger's limp hand and marches him off to the lockup.

Chapter Eighteen The Eternal Light

Emelda dances and pirouettes around the inside of the lodge, radiant with joy. At long last, revenge has been served upon the family that abused her, denied her, stole from her—and finally, killed her.

I sit with Shadow, quietly basking in her joy. We both share the deep relief of justice fulfilled. We had tasted Roger Glamier's cruelty firsthand—the savage beating Shadow endured and the scar on the back of my hand are just a few reminders of him. Justice will be served when Roger is sentenced to death, and it brings peace to know that his reign of terror is finally over.

We sit by the fire and eat the last of the smoked venison. Relief floods my mind. At last, the few remaining residents of Falandor may enjoy a reprieve from the tyranny of the Glamier family—those who took too much for too long, twisting the law with their wealth and arrogance.

That night we sleep well, undisturbed, and rise with the dawn. Shadow and I walk down the hill and into Falandor, arriving just in time to see Roger Glamier being loaded into the prison wagon.

"Excuse me for asking, sir," I say to the peacekeeper, "would it be alright to speak with the prisoner?"

"Do as you wish. He'll be taken to the city for execution tomorrow."

I step closer and look through the bars at the condemned man. I raise my scarred hand.

"Remember me?"

"Humph. You're a thief," he croaks, his voice hoarse and his face streaked with dirt and tears.

"And you are a tyrant, a bully... and a rapist."

"I am not a rapist."

"You were stopped from raping your young cousin Annmarie."

"What would you know?" he sneers, trying to regain his composure.

"I stopped you," I say, slipping on the ring and vanishing before his eyes. I reappear a second later and watch horror bloom across his face.

"You! It was you!"

"It was me, all along," I say calmly. "But you and your family were liars, thieves, and murderers long before I was ever born."

"What lies you speak."

"The first three Glamier cousins burned down the castle, stole the dagger, and murdered Emelda."

"That's a fairy tale," he snaps, turning away.

"A true one," says Emelda, materializing beside him.

Roger screams and thrashes against the wagon walls, beating his fists against the iron-bound door. But no one pays him any attention.

As I walk away, I can still hear him shouting and pounding, a man unraveling at the end of his rope.

Early the next morning, Shadow and I return to see Emelda. We laugh about what happened the day before. Her smile is brighter than ever, and her whole being begins to glow with warmth and light. The radiance grows until she is engulfed by it.

And then, the light fades—vanishes entirely.

Emelda is gone. She has gone home, into the eternal light. And I am happy for her. Happy that after so many long, restless years, she can finally rest.

I sit with Shadow on a slab of stone by the front gate of the ruined castle. Together we watch the quiet countryside, unchanged by time. Nature endures. But within me is a quiet unease—at how rapidly humanity seems to change, how easily we lose ourselves in greed and cruelty.

We sit there for a long while, savoring the silence and each other's company. I rest my hand on Shadow's shoulders. He leans into me, warm and steady.

He will stay by my side, I know, for many years to come.

The End

Don't miss out!

Visit the website below and you can sign up to receive emails whenever Trevor Finlay publishes a new book. There's no charge and no obligation.

https://books2read.com/r/B-A-DDYGE-GTYRG

BOOKS 2 READ

Connecting independent readers to independent writers.

About the Author

I grew up in New Zealand during the 1960s and '70s, surrounded by nature, animals, and endless adventures. Now living in southwest Australia, I hold a diploma in computer graphics and animation. Winters have taken me truffle hunting with my black lab; summers, to the solitude of a fire lookout tower. These real-world experiences blend with imagination to inspire the magical landscapes and curious characters that fill my stories.